KATHERINE H. BROWN

Pastries, Pies, & Poison

Ooey Gooey
Bakery Mystery
Book Two

Copyright © 2019 by Katherine Brown

Visit Katherine at
www.katherinebrownbooks.com

All rights reserved.

ISBN: 978-1-7337258-2-8

Imprint: Katherine Brown Books

No part of this book may be reproduced in any form or by any electronic or mechanical means including information storage and retrieval systems, without written permission from the author, except for the use of brief quotations in a book review.

This is a work of fiction. Names, characters, businesses, places, events, locales, and incidents are either the products of the author's imagination or used in a fictitious manner. Any resemblance to actual persons, living or dead, or actual events is purely coincidental.

~

Pastries, Pies, and Poison

Written By: Katherine Brown

Cover Design By: Breezy Reads

Piper and Sam are excited to cater their first large event – breakfast and desserts at a weekend wellness retreat at The Cove's Cabins, a new resort in a nearby town. You know what that means? Road trip!

Piper thought it sounded like the perfect opportunity to clear her head of men. With Griff confessing his feelings for her and then her old friend Landon popping back into her life, her mind and heart are in worse shape than a batch of burnt cookies.

Unfortunately for the girls, not one but two dead bodies put a damper on their working weekend.

On top of that, Griff is lying to Sam and if that isn't enough, Landon seems to have a secret that throws him into suspicion.

Can Piper sort out not only her love life but the mysterious murders as well?

~

Prologue

Saturday Afternoon

I rubbed the raised chill bumps on my arms. It was June. On the beach. On the beach in the south to be specific. It wasn't even close to cold outside, but still, I shivered. I couldn't stop thinking of that poor man. Dead. Murdered? I didn't know for sure, yet the police intended to investigate all possibilities.

I had given my statement to the deputy on the porch, followed in close succession by Sam and Landon. The questions had been brief and my responses even more so:

Did you know the victim? *No.*

Did you bake the desserts? *Yes.*

Did you serve the victim Peanut Butter Pie? *No, we were out.*

How did he get Peanut Butter Pie then? *I don't know.*

Did you have any reason to harm the victim? *No.*

Did you see the victim arguing with anyone? *No.*

The deputy told each of us not to leave The Cove's Cabins in case the police had any more questions. Landon made his way towards the rolling surf. Sam and I followed.

"Landon," I put a hand on his arm. "Are you okay?"

"Yes. No. I don't know," he shook his head.

"You said that man was your boss. What was his name?" I knew sometimes it helped to talk through things. I also felt more than a bit of curiosity at Landon's involvement with Breaking Chains. He certainly hadn't mentioned it, not that we'd had a lot of time to chat since he turned up.

"Arthur. Arthur Cole was his name."

"So, you worked for Breaking Chains?" Sam asked the obvious question for us both.

"Yeah, I'm not an office employee or anything, but my team reported to Arthur."

"I'm sorry for your loss," I squeezed his arm.

"That's the thing," Landon rubbed his jaw. "I didn't even like the guy. Don't get me wrong, he seemed like a good boss and I learned a lot from him. We weren't exactly friends though. Breaking Chains is all about helping the victims but to Arthur, it was no more than a regular business. He didn't have any real empathy or contact with the people we helped bring in off the streets. The only reason he even sat at my table was that he wanted to trade desserts with me."

"Everybody has their strengths," Sam said with a light tone. "Maybe Arthur only felt comfortable with his skills for the business end of things?"

"I guess," Landon conceded.

A scream, high-pitched and terrified, had us each whipping our necks down the beach to the left. A few other people heard and jogged toward a woman who kept screaming and scuttled backward in the sand, like a crab, as fast as she could go. She tried to stand but couldn't seem to regain her footing. She kept crawling backward, her eyes never leaving something in the edge of the waves.

"You think she saw a jellyfish or a shark or something?" I asked.

That theory evaporated seconds later.

"A body!" someone near her called. "Get the police down here, there's a body."

"Sam, hurry and get the police," I told her. Our group still huddled closest to the dining cabin and she could get there fastest. She sped toward the cabin and the officers taking statements.

I took off toward the frightened woman and the body. Don't ask me why; I spent the whole minute it took to get there asking myself what in the world I thought I could do to help. I could hear Landon's steps thudding behind me; with his longer stride, soon he overtook me.

When we got close, we saw someone attempting CPR on a woman. The figure sprawled in front of us was too still, her ebony hair tangled with seaweed and dotted with sand. Up the shore a bit, the little round man who had led the prayer at lunch sat with the lady who sighted the body first. He talked softly and nodded, patting her arm every so often to try and comfort her. Given that the screaming stopped, I'd say he was doing a good job.

The man doing CPR rocked back on his heels, shaking his head in defeat.

I gasped at the first unimpeded sight of the woman's face. I recognized her.

Chapter 1

Earlier in the Week

Knock, knock, knock.

Three sharp raps sounded at the door, causing us both to jump.

Griff and I were in my apartment.

He had driven me home after a dinner with Pastor Dan, the pastor's wife, and our families at the spa. My mind still reeled from the unexpected turn our conversation had taken. I had invited him in, expecting him to make it clear after all of the rumors going around that I was a nice girl, his sister's best friend, but nothing more to him.

Imagine my surprise when he knelt on my living room floor, telling me that he found me amazing, beautiful, kind, adorable (okay, he might have said 'stubborn in an adorable way,' but I'd take it) and saying he couldn't wait another moment to tell me how he felt.

Knock, knock, knock. The knocking at the door grew a bit louder.

Griff dropped my hand. The moment shattered and vanished. I didn't have time to process these new revelations, much less form any type of response. Saved by the door, or sabotaged, I wasn't sure.

"That's, uh, probably Sam," I shot an apologetic look his way as I got up.

Griff followed me to the door, whether out of some new desire to protect me or simply to clobber his sister for interrupting, I couldn't guess. Both thoughts made me want to giggle in a completely giddy, absolutely unacceptable way that made no sense right now.

I didn't check the peephole before opening the door. Despite my recent trauma—being kidnapped and nearly killed by a woman who had lost her marbles and decided I was a threat to her fantasy future—I felt secure and safe with Griff there behind me. Besides, that woman was gone; she couldn't hurt me anymore.

I never saw myself in need of a white knight, but having someone there with me felt good. Swinging the door wide, I experienced my second round of speechlessness in less than fifteen minutes.

"Piper?" the tanned, trim, muscular guy on my doorstep asked.

"Hi?" It came out as a question, my brain running on less than its optimum speed at this point in the evening. I tried to place this sandy-haired stranger and come up with a plausible reason for him to be at my door at this time of the evening, but I drew a blank.

"Piper, it's me. It's Landon."

I clutched at my heart in shock as recognition dawned. Too stunned to resist, I just held on as Landon scooped me up in a huge hug and spun me around the doorstep.

"Piper, are you okay? I saw the news."

"What? How are you here? What news?"

"I planned to surprise you. On the trip here to see you, I heard on the radio you were missing. Then the media said you had been kidnapped? The news showed no other headlines besides saying that someone was killed."

"A trip to see me? How did you know where I lived? How did you find me?"

The words rushed like a raging waterfall as we pinged questions back and forth at each other.

"Piper." Another voice crashed into the moment.

I turned, embarrassed at being so rude, and exclaimed, "Griff! Griff, I'm sorry, this is my friend from school. Landon, this is Griff. He's…" I trailed off in awkwardness, dreadfully aware our important discussion had been interrupted.

"I was just leaving," Griff finished. He turned to Landon. "Piper really needs her rest as you can imagine. Do you need me to give you a ride to a hotel?" Griff crossed his arms and spread his feet wide in front of my door. It became glaringly obvious he had no intentions of leaving me alone with another man at this time of night.

I would have been offended at this alpha male gesture if I wasn't tickled pink on the inside and trying not to laugh on the outside. *Whew, protective looks good on you, Griff,* I thought to myself.

Plus, he was right. This day had been too much for me. I might feel anything but tired right now, but my entire body and mind were exhausted. Anything else could wait until tomorrow.

"Thank you but no." Landon shook his head at Griff. "I have my car. You're right. I just had to make sure Piper was okay..." He turned back to me. "Would you be all right with me coming to see you tomorrow, maybe taking you to lunch so we can catch up?"

"That would be wonderful." I smiled. "Swing by the Ooey-Gooey Goodness Bakery anytime. I'm always there."

Landon gave me another big hug then turned to leave.

Griff glanced between me and the parking lot, a slight frown tugging at his mouth. "See you, Piper." He placed a soft kiss on my temple and trudged to his truck, his usual upbeat pace nowhere to be found.

I watched them both pull away, my heart aching for the conversation I botched with Griff and filled at the same time with the joy at the prospect of reuniting with Landon after so many years.

"Good night," I whispered to the quiet night.

Closing and locking my apartment door, I leaned back against it and sighed.

Apparently, tomorrow was going to be another long day.

~

Sleep didn't come without a fight; still, I did at last wrestle the pillows and my thoughts into submission. Somehow, the next morning, my eyes sprang open well before my alarm went off. I stared up into the darkness as I thought about the events of the last few days.

So much had happened. From Sam and I winning the fundraiser, to our prize of staying at the spa (the most luxurious place I had ever seen), to being stalked and sabotaged while there. Of course, it would be a very long time before being kidnapped by a lovesick lunatic ever left my mind. I shuddered, remembering the ordeal and the tragic aftermath.

Then there was Griff. And Landon.

Sigh.

I threw back the covers and headed to the kitchen. Going back to sleep clearly wasn't an option with so many thoughts playing tag in my head. So, I did what I always do. Set out to lose myself in my baking.

Now, I might have woken before the alarm, but that didn't mean I had a lot of time since I always set my alarm for the last possible minute. It's not like I have to be beauty-pageant ready to bake cookies. Alarm or no alarm, I still needed to leave for work in about half an hour. That meant I cheated a little. Yes, I snagged the can of premade crescent dough from the fridge. Don't judge me.

I slathered butter in the little triangles, rolled them up, and added more butter on top. After they had baked six or eight of the ten minutes, I would add a little more butter to help them brown. Who doesn't love butter?

For the really good part though, I found the bag of butterscotch chips. My mouth watered with anticipation as I melted the butterscotch chips, brown sugar, and water together in the microwave. The delicious aroma assaulted my senses, making me feel warm and cozy.

When the crescents were finished, I arranged them on a plate and poured the beautiful glaze over the tops. Crushing up a handful of walnuts, I sprinkled them over the glaze to add a little crunch.

Mmmm.

The warm glaze had me licking my lips, and the crescents, now bursting with flavor, melted in my mouth. Glancing at the clock, I put a few crescents in a to-go container to take to Sam and hurried to my bedroom to get dressed.

Chapter 2

I arrived at the bakery and saw Sam's car already in the lot. I used my key to unlock the back door and locked it behind me, juggling the container of crescents and my phone in the other hand.

"Morning, Piper," Sam greeted with her back still to the door. Unlike myself, Sam didn't know the meaning of the word "casual" unless it was preceded by "business." In a navy pinstriped jumper and long gold necklace, she looked completely out of place. Yet, she worked as hard as I did at running this place, comfortable in her own style and her own skin, never minding if her fancy clothes got dirty in the process.

"Morning," I greeted cheerily.

She turned from the oven and gave me a long look.

"What?" I asked. "No, really, what?"

"How are you?" she asked me, voice laced with concern. "You really can take the day off, you know."

"I'm fine!"

Sam and I co-owned and operated the Ooey-Gooey Goodness Bakery. We were also best friends, and she knew me better than anyone else. Sam raised one artfully manicured eyebrow and pursed her lips, not buying a word that came out of my mouth.

"Okay, okay. I'm exhausted and a little jumpy and confused, but I want to be here," I hated to admit the jumpy and confused part. "I'd go out of my mind at home. Plus, look." I held out the container in my hand. "I brought breakfast, and you're going to be mad if you send me home because I'll take them with me."

Relenting, Sam shook her head and took the proffered box of goodies. Cracking the lid, she closed her eyes and inhaled.

"I smell—" she drew in another deep breath "—brown sugar?"

"And butterscotch chips." I nodded. "Melted over fluffy crescents and sprinkled with walnuts."

"My gosh, why didn't you say so?" Sam opened a cabinet and pulled down two paper plates. She then made glasses of tea for each of us, and we sat down at the work island. We chewed in relative silence for several moments.

"You said you were confused," Sam latched on to one of the things I hadn't wanted to discuss. "About what?"

I lifted my tea to take a sip. Strong English breakfast tea complemented the pastries, providing a bitter note to offset the sweetness. "It's complicated. Right now, we need to get ready to open. The rest can wait."

"Hey!" Sam's eyes widened. "I almost forgot that Griff drove you home. Dish. Is he part of why you're confused? Did anything happen between you and my brother? He really started acting strange when you went missing, rambling and stressing out, his usual cool, collected self completely gone."

I ignored her.

"Piper!" Sam called as I went through the kitchen's swinging door and entered the front room, flipping on lights in the display cases as I went.

"What's the special today?" I asked as I wiped off the chalkboard and prepared to write a new dessert on it.

"Cookie Sandwich Brownies," Sam rattled off the name of our featured dessert. "You aren't getting out of talking to me that easy though."

I smiled and shrugged.

A knock on the glass door interrupted her next sentence. I checked my watch. There were still ten minutes before we opened.

"Who's the impatient guy?" Sam asked, pointing over her shoulder.

I looked up and saw Landon's searching face as he cupped his hands and peered through the door. Muffled sound filtered through the glass, the name still clear enough for Sam and me to understand.

"Piper," he called.

"Who is he?" Sam arched an eyebrow at me.

"Would you believe he's one of the confusing parts of my evening?"

"I'm definitely gonna need you to spill, and soon. Should I let him in?"

"I'll let him in if you don't mind stocking the cases. I'll just go ahead and put the open sign out, too."

"Okay." Sam disappeared back to the kitchen to grab an assortment of goodies.

"Come in," I motioned to Landon as I opened the door and waved him inside.

Hanging the *Open for Goodness* sign on the door, I turned, only to be enveloped in another giant bear hug like the one the night before.

Clank, bang. Trays of cookies rattled on the counter, and Landon let me go, turning toward the noise.

"Landon, this is my best friend and business partner, Samantha Lowe. Sam, this is my old friend Landon. We went to school together."

"Nice to meet you," Sam came around the counter to shake Landon's hand.

"My pleasure," Landon's smile encompassed us both. "I hope it's okay that I'm a bit early. Piper, I wanted to talk to you, but I got a call from my boss. I have to get back for an urgent business meeting, so it might be a few days before I'm back in town. I am coming back though," he promised, squeezing my hands.

"I understand. When do you leave?" I asked, ignoring Sam who pantomimed picking her jaw up off the floor and fanning herself behind Landon's back.

"Right now. That's why I banged on the door when I saw the closed sign." Landon ducked his head sheepishly. He had always been a bit shy in school, though I noticed he had a lot more confidence now. Something about the way he carried himself.

"Oh," I blinked as my brain tried to absorb the fact that my friend, who appeared without warning back in my life, was already disappearing again.

"Here." Sam's voice cut through the whirlwind of thoughts. "Please, take some goodies for the road."

"Thank you, Sam," Landon accepted the small box of treats with a broad smile. "Nice hair, by the way, both of you." Sam hadn't yet picked a new color and still sported a bright red underlayer. I fingered my own silver- and pale turquoise-tipped strands absentmindedly. They had been a prank on Sam originally, but I'd been debating on keeping them.

The bell over the door jingled. I looked up and saw Griff step inside. His eyes swept the room. Heat flooded my cheeks as he glanced our way and smiled. I smiled back.

Recognizing Landon, Griff gave a curt nod hello and frowned. Guilt roiled through my gut, even though I knew I had no reason to feel that way.

"I'll see you soon, Piper." Landon gave me another squeeze and waved goodbye.

Griff steered clear of us, not stopping to speak as he might have had I been alone. At the counter, Griff muttered, "The usual," to Sam in a low voice.

I approached the counter as Sam pulled a few cookies off a tray and boxed them up. Still, no idle chitchat, no discussion of today's plans or requests to try new flavors made their way past Griff's lips. I fidgeted, rocking back and forth on my toes.

Landon made his exit, the bell breaking the awkward silence.

On a whim, I hurried to the kitchen and back, tossing in the last Butterscotch-Glazed Crescent.

"You make crescents now?" Griff asked.

"Not the crescent, the glaze. It's a new recipe. Let me know what you think."

"Okay, thanks."

The bell jingled as two or three of our morning regulars trickled in.

"Griff, listen," I started.

"I've got to go. I'll be out of town working for a few days." Turning, he left without another word—not even a goodbye to Sam.

"See." She pointed after him. "I told you he was acting odd. He didn't even try to weasel extra cookies out of us."

Chapter 3

We had just sent Frank, our last customer for the moment, off with his weekly Apple Fritter Muffin when Gladys entered. I noticed she still had her gorgeous manicure from the spa last week as I looked sadly down at my own nails. My struggle and the narrow escape from my captor on the beach last week meant more wear and tear than the polish could handle. Now scrubbed clean with nail polish remover, my nails were plain and ordinary once again.

"Hello, girls." Gladys smiled and greeted us in her normal cheerful way. "Do you have any coffee left?"

"Coming right up." Sam smiled as she reached for a mug.

"How are Jack and Drew?" I asked. Gladys had an unconventional hobby, a form of wood carving, only she carved faces into trees. Jack and Drew were two palm trees in her backyard she had taken to conversing with when bored.

"Growing every day. Thank you for asking, Piper."

"Here you are," Sam sat a steaming mug of coffee and a pitcher of cream in front of Gladys.

"And what about a Cranberry Orange Muffin this morning?" I offered.

"Don't mind if I do." Gladys accepted the plate. "Now, what did I miss?"

"What do you mean?"

"All the juicy details, of course. Griff drove you home, did he not?"

"You haven't missed a thing," Sam told her. "Piper wouldn't tell me anything this morning. But look, now we have a nice break, and she can go ahead and fill us in."

I stuck my tongue out at my friend. She pulled out a chair at the table and patted it for me to sit down, taking the seat beside it. I knew she had the tenacity to wait me out, so I sat. May as well tell them both together before I had to say anything twice.

"Fine. Last night, while Griff and I were talking, Landon showed up at my apartment."

"Who's Landon?" Gladys interrupted around a bite of her muffin, crumbs sprinkling her napkin.

"Whoops." Sam shrugged. "Maybe you missed just a little bit." She held her finger and thumb close together, indicating it was just a small amount.

"Let me start at the beginning," I huffed with a shake of my head. "Griff did drive me home. I invited him in because he said he needed to talk to me. I assumed that with all of the drama in the news about my kidnapping and rumors it had to do with a catfight over the most eligible bachelor—him—that he wanted to make it clear that we were just friends."

"This girl is clueless, isn't she?" Gladys rolled her eyes and shared an exasperated look with Sam who nodded.

I didn't tell them I had also assumed that Deidra, Griff and Sam's mother, had put him up to speaking with me. That woman hated me; she thought I was a terrible influence on her daughter by roping her into a bakery and away from the life of poise and politics that Deidra envisioned for her. To have it rumored I might now be involved with Griff—well, I would expect it to send Deidra into conniptions.

"Anyway," I continued, ignoring the peanut gallery, "I invited Griff inside and changed into pajamas while I tried to get my thoughts straight. I apologized to him and let him know I was sorry about the mess and that I would, somehow, let everyone know that he just looked out for me as a friend, that we weren't involved." I rolled my eyes and admitted the rest. "As you apparently may have guessed, I had it all wrong. Griff told me he didn't think of me as a friend. That he thought I was amazing and talented and all kinds of things. He told me that when I went missing, his biggest fear was that he would never get to tell me how he felt."

Sam and Gladys leaned forward, waiting.

"And then?" Sam demanded.

"Then someone knocked on the door." I caught them up on the whole awkward doorstep situation.

Gladys was intrigued by the mention of Landon. "Why did he come to see you?"

"I don't know."

"Why didn't you ask him last night?" Sam wanted to know.

I chuckled. "I didn't get to. Your brother didn't give me a chance. Griff nearly escorted Landon from the door. Told him I needed rest. He even offered to take him to a hotel." I started laughing, thinking back on the scene, but sobered when I realized now both Griff and Landon were gone and I hadn't finished the important conversations with either of them.

"Landon got called back to work for a meeting. I don't even know where he works," I realized aloud as I filled Gladys and Sam in. "Then

Griff came in this morning and told Sam and me that he was working out of town for a few days."

"He didn't say where exactly he was going either," Sam threw in.

"So, you and Griff didn't finish talking?" Gladys looked disappointed.

"And she never got to speak with Landon about whatever reason he came here," Sam pointed out.

"Right," I leaned back in my chair and massaged my fingers through my hair. "They're both a mystery, but especially Landon. It's been at least six years since I've seen him. See now why I'm tired and confused? Who knows when I'll get to speak with either of them again?"

"You need chocolate," Sam decided, getting up. She foraged through the display case and came back with an Almond Dark Chocolate Drizzle, two actually, one for me and one for Gladys. "Relax for a little bit. I'm going to go put some more cookies into the oven."

Poised to bite into the ooey-gooey deliciousness in front of me, I stopped with my hand halfway to my mouth as the bell jingled, announcing another customer. Stifling a sigh, I put the cookie down and started to stand, but Gladys reached a hand out to stop me.

"I can take an order or two. You deserve a break, Piper," she admonished. "Most people wouldn't have come to work today. Most people probably wouldn't even come to work the rest of this week for that matter."

"Thank you." I accepted her offer of help and sat back down. I wanted to argue, but I knew she was right. A fifteen-minute break might be just the trick, and if not, then surely the cookie would help.

I ate my cookie and watched as Gladys took the order of a young woman who was running late to work. Gladys complimented her style and shoes as she made change from the register. The woman left smiling, happier and less harried than when she arrived.

Next came a man looking to buy something special for his wife. He mentioned it was for a birthday surprise.

Gladys told him you could never go wrong with chocolate. "Unless she has an allergy. Does she have any allergies?" she asked him. When he said no, Gladys reached into the display case and emerged with a square of the day's special—a Cookie Sandwich Brownie—and an extra-large Chocolate Chunk Cookie.

I ate Gladys's cookie too as I continued to watch her work her magic. For Grandpa Rex, an elderly gentleman who stopped in a few times a week to buy cookies for his grandkids, she talked him into adding a Butterscotch Oatmeal Cookie for himself to his order.

"You're a natural," I told Gladys when she finally rejoined me at the small table. "I might just hire you the next time I want to go on vacation."

Sam came through the swinging doors then and laughed.

"What is this? Piper talking about vacation? Yeah, right. And purple pigs make golden bacon," she teased. "You never take vacations."

"I went to the spa," I pointed out, crossing my arms.

"Only because we won, and I practically had to drag you," she argued.

The bakery phone rang, ceasing our debate. Sam answered on the second ring.

"Piper, I need you to come here, please," she requested after speaking to the caller for a moment.

Getting up from the table, I tossed my napkin in the trash before joining Sam behind the counter.

"Piper, the customer on the phone wants to know if we cater," she whispered as she covered the mouthpiece.

"I'm sure one of us can handle delivery while the other watches the store. We catered for your mother, and that went well." It surprised me a little that she was even asking.

"No, they want to know if we will cater the dessert bar at a two-day event and remain in residence to make sure it is stocked for the whole weekend."

"Oh." I chewed on my bottom lip. "I don't know…" After a moment's thought, I finally said, "Ask them when they need an answer and tell them we will let them know." I didn't want to miss out on an opportunity; however, after being gone four days last week, I feared how much business shutting down another weekend would lose us.

"I asked them to send an email with the details. They need an answer tomorrow," Sam told me as she hung up the phone.

"What event is it anyway?"

"You won't believe me when I tell you."

Chapter 4

"Breaking Chains?" I repeated in surprise.

"That's right." Sam nodded. "Breaking Chains has a corporate wellness retreat coming up only one town away, in Lion's Cove. Since we are so close and raised so much money for the fundraiser, they thought we might be interested in catering the event."

"Wow! That's incredible. I wonder how they knew we were nearby though? I thought all of the fundraiser money was sent through Sandy Shores Evangelical Church to the Breaking Chains organization?"

"I don't know. Still, I'm not sure we can leave the bakery for another two days. Customers might resent the inconvenience."

"And on a weekend, one of our busiest times," I agreed.

"Yeah. About that." Sam bit her bottom lip, a sign that she really didn't want to tell me something.

"What is it?"

"We really need the weekend business. Funneling so many of our own profits into the fundraiser last week really depleted our accounts. I counted on this weekend to put us back on track."

"How bad?"

"If we aren't open this weekend, I'm afraid we'll come up short on the electric bill," she admitted.

I cringed. Not good. I had no idea finances had gotten so low. Sam handled the accounting side of things because she excelled at math and business. Me, the only math I like is when you add up a bunch of ingredients and the result is multiplying cookies.

"You can do it," Gladys put two thumbs up from across the room. "You can do the catering and keep the bakery open. You were about to hire an assistant, remember?" she asked with a wink and a flourish of hands indicating herself. "I can watch the bakery."

I mulled it over. Sam shrugged her shoulders.

Tempting indeed, but I knew Gladys couldn't handle all of the baking and manage the counter at the same time, no matter how impressive her customer service might be. It required at least two people. We had a really big dilemma and not a lot of time to figure it out.

"Girls, this is up to you, but I really would love to help out if you decide to take the job," Gladys insisted from her seat, making no apologies for listening. "I had so much fun this morning behind the counter," she added with a sincere smile.

The bell jingled over the door. I glanced at the clock. Ten forty-five a.m. The lunch crowd was about to hit, and yes, just as many people choose to eat cookies and pastries for lunch as choose to eat fast food. Personally, I commend them for their good taste.

"We will have to discuss this later." I moved to the counter to help the customer.

"Okay. I'm going to head on home now," Gladys informed us. "Why don't you girls come over for supper and let me know your decision?"

"Sounds excellent!" Sam agreed wholeheartedly. Her excitement came from the thought of a home-cooked meal more than a solution to our current problem. Beyond baking, my friend wasn't much of a cook. Before we were roommates in college, I'm pretty sure she was living on burnt toast or dining out at posh restaurants.

"That will be great," I thanked Gladys. "We'll see you around seven thirty."

~

"Piper," Sam called a few hours later. "It looks like we are almost out of Spectacular Sprinkle Cookies and Chocolate Chip Cookies."

"Wow!" I took a peek in the display case. Sam was right. "You know, I noticed we had more kids in here today, with parents or babysitters. I guess they're looking for little treats now that summer has arrived. I'll go make some more dough to bake if you want to watch the counter for a bit?"

"I've got it, go ahead," Sam agreed.

I inhaled deeply as I stepped into our kitchen. White and blue marbled countertops gleamed, their colors mimicking the ocean and bringing an immediate sense of happiness. Tan cabinets lined every wall, and the deep walk-in freezer near the back sent a thrill through me. I took a moment to bask in how blessed I was—owning my dream bakery with my best friend in the world, bringing little bites of pleasure to our customers who were fast becoming friends, living in this beautiful beachside town. *Thank you for this amazing life,* I said a quick prayer in my head as I gathered up an armful of mixing bowls, spoons, and measuring cups.

"Now, where is that recipe book?" I muttered. I hunted through a few more cabinets. Chocolate Chip Cookies I knew by heart; they would be baking in no time, but Spectacular

Sprinkle Cookies were new, and I wanted to double-check a few things.

"Gotcha!" I shouted at last, finding it tucked away in a drawer.

"Are you yelling for me?" Sam asked, popping her head through the swinging door.

"No, just talking to myself," I admitted. After discovering Gladys conversed with palm trees, I didn't feel the least bit silly for talking to myself.

"Okay then." Sam rolled her eyes and left me to my continued mutterings.

Scanning through the recipe, I found what I needed to know. Similar to a brown sugar cookie, these Spectacular Sprinkle Cookies called for almond extract as the secret ingredient. Just a drop though, it's strong stuff. Pulling together the last items I would need onto the countertop, I preheated the oven to three hundred fifty degrees and got started. I always prefer to melt the butter first because it makes combining it with the sugar much easier. After mixing those together, I added the egg and the almond extract. Flour and baking soda were next, mixing them in slow turns to form a soft dough. One drop of blue and red food coloring stirred in with a light hand, just enough to create swirls without coloring the whole dough. Forming the dough into balls, I rolled each ball in a bowl of sprinkles then placed them on the parchment paper-covered cookie sheet and pressed them down slightly with the bottom of a glass. Voila! These colorful, crunchy masterpieces were ready to bake.

"You bake up nice and soft now," I told the cookies as I closed the oven door on them.

Chocolate Chip Cookies took even less time to mix up. I made two batches and added crushed almonds to one bowl. I looked forward to tasting the Chocolate Chip and Almond Cookies. They had been a specific request by a customer and something that inspired my Almond Dark Chocolate Drizzle recipe when we were out of walnuts.

"How's it going?" I asked as I popped back into the front of the store to see if Sam needed anything. I found her waving out the last customer, leaving the two of us alone again.

"Great." Sam smiled. "Piper, we've had two birthday party orders for next week. They both want two dozen Spectacular Sprinkle Cookies."

"Wow!"

"Do you think we should take dessert to Gladys's house tonight?"

"Good idea. What do you think we should take though?" I stooped to look through the display case, searching for inspiration.

"I have an idea, but it isn't really a summer dessert."

"Dessert is dessert and desserts are good, at least that's my philosophy," I told her as I stood back up.

"Okay." Sam laughed. "I've been wanting to try Pecan Pie Cookies with chocolate drizzled over them. I think they could be a hit if I make them right."

"They sound delicious! I love pecan pie, especially chocolate pecan pie."

"Thanks, I found a recipe online the other day," Sam admitted. "I have tons of pecans left in my freezer and wanted to get rid of them."

"After I get the cookies out of the oven in a few minutes, we can switch places, and you can run home to collect your pecans for baking cookies while I watch the counter."

"Perfect, thanks, Piper!"

The timer buzzed. I retrieved the cookies from the oven and set them on racks to cool, helping myself to a sample of course. "Mmmm." Chocolate oozed from every bite, and there was just the right crunch from the almonds. The cookies were complete ooey-gooey goodness, just like our name promised.

The rest of the afternoon flew by. Baking might be my passion, but I also enjoy chatting with our customers. Around five p.m., two teenage girls came in. Ordering tea and a plate of Butterscotch Oatmeal Cookies, they sat down with a newspaper and used a red pen to circle things in the classifieds section.

"These are delish," the blonde girl licked her lips. She wore a flamboyant orange and pink striped top, long and flowy, over tan leggings.

"Yeah. I bet they would be incredible with peanut butter chips added, too," the second girl chimed in. She was a bit shorter, with long brown hair. She wore skinny jeans and a pale-yellow tee. I watched as she continued to chew thoughtfully on the cookie before she spoke again. "Or even peanut butter in the cookie itself. I wonder how good that would be?"

Not a bad idea, I thought to myself. Wandering over to their table, I offered to get them more tea.

"That would be great, thanks." The blonde smiled.

"I'm Piper," I introduced myself to the girls as I returned with their glasses of tea.

"I'm Millie," the blonde placed a hand on her chest before waving it at the dark-haired girl with the cookie ideas. "This is Victoria." Victoria smiled and continued to comb the newspaper.

"Victoria," I began, "I couldn't help but hear your thoughts about the cookies."

"I'm sorry," she said as embarrassment bloomed in her cheeks. "Your cookies are delicious, don't pay any attention to me."

"No, I loved your ideas!" I assured her. "Actually, I couldn't help noticing you were searching the paper. Any chance you're looking for work this summer?"

"Yes, ma'am." She nodded. "Millie and I both need jobs. We want to earn money to buy electric scooters."

"Please, call me Piper, not ma'am. Can you bake?" I crossed my fingers behind my back, waiting for the pivotal answer to this half-baked idea of mine.

"Victoria can," Millie smiled. Then frowned. "I'm…not so good in the kitchen."

"I see." I nodded and chewed thoughtfully on my lip. "I need to talk with my partner for a moment. Do you girls think you could wait here at least ten more minutes?"

Chapter 5

That evening, Sam and I pulled up in front of Gladys's bright yellow bungalow at a few minutes before seven thirty.

"It cracks me up," I pointed between the bungalow and the car. "Sam, I think you and Gladys shopped together because your car and her house match perfectly."

"Ha-ha." Sam grabbed the container of Pecan Pie Cookies from the back seat, and we ambled up the walkway.

Gladys opened the door before we could knock. "Come in, come in."

"Something smells wonderful," I breathed in the mingling aromas.

"I hope you're ready to eat." Gladys smiled as she led us down the short hallway to the dining nook off the kitchen.

Sam's stomach growled as if on cue, and we all laughed.

"Have a seat," Gladys told us. "I'll just grab the rolls out of the oven."

"Gladys!" Sam exclaimed as we stared at the heaping platters of food filling the small table.

"You didn't need to go to so much trouble for us." I couldn't believe my eyes.

"Nonsense," she huffed. "It's been too long since I have had anyone around to cook a nice meal for, and I decided it might as well be a good one. I enjoyed doing it," she insisted.

Eyeballing all of the food, I tried to determine where I would start.

"Here we go." Gladys brought a basket of fresh bread rolls and added it to the table. "We have Beef Bourguignon, Ratatouille, French Onion Soup, radishes with butter, and rolls."

"Gladys, this isn't a home-cooked meal, it's a French restaurant on your table," I shook my head in amazement.

"How in the world did you get all of this done?" Sam asked, spreading her napkin in her lap.

"Just a little cooking, that's all." Gladys sat down and shook out her own napkin. "Now let's say the blessing and eat before everything gets cold."

~

"These are delicious, Sam," I moaned as I finished off my second Pecan Pie Cookie. We were sitting on the back porch, enjoying the night's cool breeze while we ate dessert.

"Piper," Sam broached, "do you want to tell Gladys your plan that would allow us to cater the corporate wellness retreat for Breaking Chains?"

"So, you've decided?" Gladys asked.

"We definitely want to cater the event," I said, "but it will depend on a trial run of my plan before Sam or I will call Breaking Chains and commit. We may have to ask them for one more day to decide. Two teenage girls came into the bakery today, and both were scouring the newspaper for jobs. I overheard one of them, Victoria, coming up with cookie ideas that sounded tasty. Turns out, she has some kitchen skills, according to her friend Millie."

"Okay," Gladys nodded her head. "So, what are you thinking?"

"Well," I considered my thoughts and spoke slowly, "I think we should do a test run for a day or two this week with you, Millie, and Victoria working in the bakery. If we train the girls and they seem able to do a good job, then the three of you could watch the bakery during our catering job. Gladys, you would be wonderful working the counter given your people skills and friendly personality, we already saw that."

"How fun!" Gladys clapped.

"We might need you to check in on Victoria or help her from time to time, also." I continued laying out the plan. "Millie admits she has no cooking skills; however, she is willing to do all of the cleaning tasks and take a spell at the counter anytime you need a break."

"What do you think?" Sam asked. "Would you like to do a test run tomorrow?"

"I am flattered." Gladys nodded. "I do have one important question though."

"What's that?" I asked.

"Do I get to be the official taste tester?"

Sam and I laughed.

"Absolutely," Sam told Gladys. "You should taste everything that is baked while we are gone. Victoria and Millie are welcome to sample everything as well."

"I'm in!" A smile stretched from ear to ear. Gladys turned. "You hear that, Drew? I've got a new job tomorrow."

I shook my head as Gladys patted the little palm tree. Oh boy. At least there were no trees or plants in the bakery for Gladys to personify.

"So, at least that solves one of your problems, Piper," Gladys spoke, turning back to me.

"One of them?" I frowned. "What's the other one?"

"Sorting out things with Griff and Landon, of course!"

Sigh. And I had hoped not to think about them at all.

"There's nothing to sort out. Sam and I will be busy getting ready for the catering event, training the girls, not to mention Griff and Landon will be gone for several days anyway."

"I still can't believe I never guessed that Griff had feelings for you." Sam smirked. "I thought I had my brother all figured out. I guess I was wrong."

"And you, Piper? I could see the first day I saw you two together that you would be a cute couple." Gladys winked. "Now a man other than Griff has come into your life with obvious affection for you. Do you know what you want?"

"Yes," I declared, startling them both. Sam tilted her head at me while Gladys leaned forward in her chair. "I want…another cookie!"

"Phooey!" Gladys slapped her knee. "You can pretend it isn't a big deal if you want to, but you can't fool me."

Handing me the plate of cookies, Sam shook her head. "Here," she offered, "and when you are ready to think about this seriously, I hope you know I'll be happy with whatever you decide."

I nodded and chewed my cookie thoughtfully. Before long, Sam and I took our leave.

Chapter 6

Flour coated the kitchen. It was literally everywhere. I blinked. *Deep breaths,* I told myself.

"Piper, I am soooo sorry. I should have watched where I was going," Victoria apologized as she went through the futile effort of wiping flour-covered hands on her flour-coated apron. Neither looked any cleaner for the experience.

"No, it's my fault," Millie insisted, shaking the flour from her body like a dog shaking off bathwater. "I forgot where the dishrags for cleaning the countertops were at, and I bent down to look in the cabinet. I should have told Victoria I was there, then she wouldn't have tripped over me."

Behind me, a low chuckle commenced. In seconds, it erupted into full-blown laughter, followed by wheezing. I turned.

"I'm sorry." Gladys wiped tears from her eyes as she drew a deep breath. She doubled over in laughter again. "Look at this mess." She waved her hands at the scene and continued to shake with mirth.

I looked back at the girls. Millie was now trying to blink flour from her eyelashes, the rapid movements of her eyelids making her look crazy. Victoria scraped at the cabinet with her arm, raking flour into a trash bag. Silence finally reigned when the large metal bowl that Victoria had been carrying the bag of flour in finally clanked to a stop in the corner, ceasing its spinning at last.

Sam stepped into the kitchen just then—she had stayed behind to ring up a customer when Gladys and I rushed to find out what happened to cause such a commotion. She took one look at the room and escaped back out front.

Before I spoke, I counted to ten. Three times.

"It's okay. Millie, grab the broom, please. Victoria, just wipe that flour onto the floor. We can sweep it all up, it's fine." I plastered on a smile, hoping to assure the girls that I wasn't angry, at the same time praying that leaving the bakery to cater for the weekend wasn't an error in judgment. *What was I thinking, leaving teenagers in my kitchen?*

Millie spun and rushed to the broom closet. Victoria nodded and swept a giant mound of flour off the counter where it caught the circulating air and fanned out to cover us all. Gladys nearly collapsed in a renewed bout of laughing and coughing.

"On second thought," I told Millie as I dusted flour from my face, "get the vacuum and the hose attachment. Nobody else moves."

Eventually, the kitchen was spotless again. The girls were hard workers; I would give them credit for that. Overall, the rest of the day went smoothly, and there were no more mishaps.

"Victoria is a fast learner," I told Sam as we shared a plate of cookies in the café that afternoon. "And her ideas for tweaks on cookies are creative. I'm going to let her mix up a batch of whatever she wants this afternoon to put in the walk-in fridge for tomorrow."

"That's great. Do you still think we can leave the Ooey-Gooey Bakery for the catering job?" Sam made a face, and I also cringed. There was likely still flour in my hair.

"Yes, in spite of the flour fiasco today, I think things will be fine." I looked over at the register as I said this, watching as Gladys cooed at a young baby and suggested a Triple Chocolate to a haggard young mom. "Gladys is a natural, Victoria is smart and eager. I wasn't sure about hiring Millie, but she is happy to do whatever cleaning is needed as long as she's earning money for her scooter. That will be a huge time-saver for Gladys and Victoria." I put as much confidence into my voice as I could muster.

In truth, I would be surprised if I didn't have a panic attack that the bakery was in the hands of someone other than me for two days. Some might call me a control freak; I prefer the term highly responsible.

"Yeah, I feel better that there will be three of them here and not just two. The baking, stocking, cleaning, and counter sales are a lot of jobs to split between two people. Remember how long it took us to get the hang of it?" Sam laughed and shook her head.

"Oh gosh, yes!" I nodded. "It surprised me when we lasted the whole first week."

"And even though our only customer the first two days was Griff, we still nearly ran out of cookies because we didn't mix any up the night before our second day. We couldn't bake them fast enough!"

"We've come a long way since then." I smiled at the memory. Griff's employees came in and bought everything we had on day one. Later, one of them told Sam that Griff had threatened to fire them if they went anywhere else during their lunch break. We never did figure out if he was joking or not; neither of us had the heart to ask Griff. "I think I came to work wearing the same clothes three days in a row because I stayed up each night working on new recipes."

"You did," Sam remembered, "but I didn't notice because I was having a hair crisis. I fell asleep trying to add blonde streaks and ended up with orange-highlighter colors staining my hair and head."

"That explains your ballcap days!"

We chuckled, and soon Gladys joined us, having helped the last customer and sent them on their way, a sack of cookies in hand and a smile on their face.

"Girls," Gladys addressed us, "what do you think? Can you trust us with your baby while you work the weekend away?"

Sam and I looked at each other. Sam nodded.

"Definitely," I answered.

"I'm going to call Breaking Chains right now and let them know," Sam pulled her phone from her purse.

"Wonderful! Do you mind if I take off a little early today?" Gladys asked, glancing at her watch. She had been checking it for the last hour.

"Go right ahead," I told her. "I hope we didn't keep you from anything?"

"Not at all. I just have a little cooking to do."

"Okay, we'll see you tomorrow then."

"See you. Bye, Sam," she mouthed toward Sam who had moved a few feet away to place the phone call. Sam waved goodbye and smiled.

The bell jingled as Gladys went out and then again as the next customer came inside.

"Hi, Flo," my smile a little too wide. I hoped my surprise at seeing her in the bakery didn't show on my face. Flo owned Flo's Flowers, the business next door to Ooey-Gooey Goodness Bakery, and used to be a regular customer. Flo had stopped purchasing from us after we won the fundraiser contest last week.

"Good afternoon, Piper. I'd like half a dozen Blueberry Scones, please."

"Of course. Let me box those up for you." I turned, raising my eyebrow at Sam once Flo was behind me, and retrieved a to-go box from beneath the register. There were only seven Blueberry Scones left in the glass display case, so I put all of them in the box for Flo. I wasn't one to hold a grudge, and it was nice to have her business again. Ringing up the total for six scones, I hoped she would see the extra pastry as my gesture of goodwill. I put Flo's money in the drawer and handed over the box.

"Enjoy," I told her sincerely.

Chapter 7

Sam came and found me after she got off the phone. "It's all set. Breaking Chains will have us stay the whole weekend to cover breakfast and the dessert bar after lunch and dinner."

"Who is cooking lunch and dinner?"

"Those meals will be catered by a seafood restaurant local to the area. Don't worry, they cook everything and then bring it in warmers. The kitchen will be restricted just for our use."

"What makes you think I was worried about that?" I asked with mock offense.

"First, because you always worry, Piper. Need I remind you of the spa outfit dilemma?" Sam joked. I stuck out my tongue, which she took as a sign to continue. "And second, because your forehead was pinched in all those little worry lines."

"Fine. Thank you for making all of the arrangements and for checking on the setup." I grabbed a notepad and pen from beside the register. "Now, what do you need me to do?"

Several lists later—yes, I may or may not have a list obsession—we had a plan to tackle the catering weekend. Sam would train Millie, I would train Victoria, and Gladys would be here to supervise and help when we left. Her five-star French meal for supper was proof enough she could handle things in a kitchen if need be.

"Millie," I called through the swinging door. The girl pushed her blonde hair behind her ears, mopping sweat from her face, but smiled cheerfully at me.

"Yes?"

"Sam's going to show you how to do a quick check of inventory. We don't want Victoria to run out of supplies, and you can help keep track of ingredients for her."

"Sounds good," she agreed with a quick nod.

"Follow me." Sam motioned. They ventured into the walk-in pantry, Sam with a clipboard and Millie with a determined look on her face. I opened the café door and looked around. The sidewalks were empty, so we probably had a few minutes between customers. I made my way into the kitchen where Victoria was scribbling ferociously on a tablet with a short red stylus.

"Hi, Victoria, how's it going?" I asked, sliding onto a tall stool next to her at the work island.

"Piper! I have so many ideas that I don't even know where to start. How do you know when you have a good recipe?"

"I don't. No, really!" I insisted as she looked at me with a *yeah, right* face. "I don't know whether the cookies will be good or not until I bake them."

"Everything you make is so delicious though. I'm afraid mine will be horrible."

"I can't very well put the recipes that flop on the menu, now can I?" I laughed.

I understood how she felt. I remembered my first awe of cakes that looked like works of art when I was a girl eating in fancy restaurants. It was years before baking became my dream job, but when it did, I suffered from comparison crisis—I couldn't bake a thing at first for fear it would never live up to the delicious desserts I had tasted by others. I didn't want Victoria to feel paralyzed from her own anxiety.

"Trust me, Victoria, there have been some batters that went straight into the trash. Take the Spectacular Sprinkle Cookies, for instance. The first time I made those, I used twice as much almond extract as they really needed. I almost gave up on them, but they were so beautiful I decided to give the flavors a second shot. It worked. With just a hint of the almond, the cookies became delectable to not only the eye but the mouth."

"So, what you're telling me is that you aren't going to tell me what to bake. I just have to screw it up myself and go from there?" Victoria gave a little sigh.

"Exactly. Don't worry though, I know you'll do great. Trust your instincts. Maybe even start small, look through my recipes, and put your own spin on one like you were talking about in the café yesterday."

"You wouldn't mind?" She laid the stylus down and took the recipe binder I handed her.

"Not at all. I would be flattered. Then tomorrow we can work together on some things and you can ask me questions."

"Okay, thanks. I'll let you know when I finish something new today."

The bell jingled out front.

"I'll leave you to it then. And, Victoria?" I waited until I had her full attention. "Relax, have fun." She gave a small smile and a nod. Leaving her to the creative cyclone that I knew would occur with a new recipe, I returned to the counter to help customers.

"Pastor Dan!" I greeted the man perusing display cases in the café. "How are you?"

"Hello there, Piper. I'm doing wonderful." The middle-aged man smiled back at me. The pastor at Sandy Shores Evangelical Church, Pastor Dan had been very grateful for the fundraising efforts of all the businesses. As the winners, Sam and I received a week at the O Heavenly Day Spa operated by the church, and there I met Pastor Dan over dinner. Kind, warm, and full of laughter, Pastor Dan quickly became a friend.

"And how is Nora?" I asked, remembering Pastor Dan's sweet wife.

"She's fine, thank you. Actually, she's the reason I came today. She said she wanted a few of your Lemon Basil Cookies."

"Excellent. Let me get a bag. Three or four?"

"I think four would be plenty. It's just the two of us, after all."

I nodded. *I wonder what the pastor's sweet wife would think if she knew I ate four cookies just for brunch.* Sam and Millie stepped out of the back at that moment, obviously having finished in the pantry.

"Pastor Dan!" Sam strode over and gave the pastor a hug. "How good to see you again so soon."

"And you, Samantha." Pastor Dan smiled. "Now, what's this? Your hair is still the same color! What would your mother say?" he asked with a twinkle in his eye.

"Only the Lord knows." Sam winked. "You better not tell her you saw it the same color twice, or she might get her hopes up that I'm 'growing to be sensible at last.'"

We all three laughed. Deidra, who also happened to be the town's first lady, still wore pearls, heels, and suit dresses every day of her life. She was appalled that her only daughter wore gaudy hair colors and less conservative outfits. Don't even get me started on how stricken she was when she learned Sam and I were opening the Ooey-Gooey Goodness Bakery. Needless to say, it hadn't helped an already strained mother-daughter relationship.

"Pastor Dan, have you met Millie?" Sam asked as she gestured Millie to come forward.

"I don't believe so. A pleasure to meet you, young lady. Are you working here, too?"

"For a little while." Millie's blonde hair bounced with her energy as she nodded. "Piper and Sam are letting me clean and manage supplies for the weekend since they will be gone. My friend and I are going to buy electric scooters."

"Oh? Had such a blast at the spa, you ladies can't stay away?" the pastor asked Sam and me merrily.

"If only." Sam smiled.

Personally, I wasn't quite ready to go back to the place where snakes slithered in, steam room doors stuck shut, and a loony lady kidnapped me all in the same weekend. *Though the pedicure was magnificent*, I caught myself thinking.

"No." I shook my head. "Sam and I have been invited to cater a corporate wellness event for Breaking Chains."

"That's magnificent! Congratulations."

"Thank you. It is going to be a lot of work, but when I think of the things the employees of Breaking Chains must see, the cruel and dirty reality of human trafficking, the abused children, the hopeless victims—well, it will be a joy to bring them a little bit of goodness in return."

"I only wish we could do more," Sam added. "Still, it is an honor they chose the Ooey-Gooey Bakery since our business is so new. Wish us luck."

"You don't need luck, Sam. You and Piper will be blessed as you are a blessing to others. And remember, when possible, refresh the people you meet with more than refreshments." Pastor Dan took his leave on those words of wisdom, waving to the three of us as he headed home to the missus with a sack of Lemon Basils.

"He seemed nice," Millie noted. "What is Breaking Chains, by the way?"

Sam told Millie about the goal of Breaking Chains to raise awareness of human trafficking and prevent it by educating the public on signs to look for and providing support to law enforcement when requested, such as victim relief counseling and advocates when victims were identified.

The bell jingled, marking the entrance of another customer. Flo again. *Odd*, I thought.

I left the counter to speak with Flo. She had halted just inside the door and seemed unable to make up her mind about coming in or not.

"Hey, Flo," I spoke casually, worried she might bolt for some reason. "I hope nothing was wrong with your order?"

"No, nothing wrong. Look, Piper, I..."

"Would you like to sit down with a coffee or something?" I asked as her words dried up.

"No, thank you. I just need to say this." She took a breath. I braced myself. Were insults headed my way? More accusations that Sam's parents influenced our fundraising win? I sincerely hoped this wouldn't be a subject of contention forever.

"I'm sorry."

I stood there, hearing her words but not fully processing them.

"I'm sorry," Flo apologized again. "I'm sorry for the way I treated you and Sam after the contest."

"Oh! Flo, it's okay." I brushed off the apology but stopped when Flo held up a hand.

"I was jealous," Flo continued. "And it is not okay. I really wanted to win that trip to the spa because I've been having these back pains lately. I hoped a massage would help, but I really can't afford to go get one because sales have been slow. I'm sorry for being so petty. It truly is wonderful the money your bakery raised, that all of our businesses raised, really, and I hope you and Sam will forgive me."

"Of course, we forgive you!" I stepped forward and hugged Flo, surprising us both. Not usually a hugger, I decided to blame it on Nora's and Pastor Dan's kind influence.

"I'd like to continue my weekly scone order, though maybe just one would be better for me," Flo added.

"Great, we will bring you a fresh scone tomorrow morning." I smiled.

"Thanks. I better get back to the shop." Flo turned to leave. "Would be a shame to miss a customer, you know."

I watched Flo walk the short length of the sidewalk and enter her shop next door, pondering her problem. She seemed really worried about business being down. I wondered if there was some way that we could help her. Lost in thought, I didn't realize that Sam had set Millie to another task and sidled up next to me.

"What was that all about?" Sam asked, making me jump.

"Flo stopped by to apologize. She wants to resume ordering baked goods, though she said just one scone instead of her normal three will do."

"To apologize for what? For not placing orders after we won the contest?"

"For the attitude behind it, really. She says she was jealous and angry." I reiterated the short conversation with Sam, including Flo's low sales and inability to afford a massage for her pain.

"Poor Flo!" Sam's big heart showed immediately. "I wish she had asked for help, I'm sure I could have spoken to someone at the spa for her. Pastor Dan might have even recommended they get her in for an appointment half-price as a contest participant."

"I didn't think of that," I admitted. "I wondered more along the lines of what we could do now to help boost the flower shop sales."

"Hmm. I guess all of the spring weddings are over. Besides a few birthdays and anniversaries, what might people order flowers for in the summer?"

"Good question."

Before we could continue that train of thought, it was derailed by a squeal and a yell.

"Piper! OMG, Piper," Victoria squealed with her head peeking out of the door to the kitchen. "Hurry!"

Oh gosh, not more flour everywhere, I thought. *Yikes! Or worse, what if the kitchen flooded or the oven caught fire?* Scenario after scenario flashed through my brain as I sprinted to the kitchen. I cast my eyes around and saw—nothing. No flour, no water, no smoke.

"What? What is it?" I asked, tamping down the panic in my chest.

"They're perfect!" Victoria exclaimed.

"What?" I repeated.

"The cookies. Try them." She held out a sheet pan. "They turned out better than I expected."

Cookies. She was yelling about cookies. *Whew, okay, good deal.* I mentally shrugged, knowing I would do the same thing. I snagged a cookie from the tray and bit off a mouthful. I closed my eyes as I traced each flavor flitting across my tongue.

"Peanut butter, oats, butterscotch, chocolate. Wow!" I ticked them off out loud. Opening my eyes, I saw Victoria doing a silent little dance. I gently took the cookie tray from her. "Wouldn't want your beautiful creation to go flying," I pointed out, moving the tray to the counter. She stood grinning back at me.

"Do you really like them?" she asked.

"Yes." I nodded. "Tell me about them."

Chapter 8

Friday.

The day before the weekend catering event.

I wiped my sweaty palms on my cargo pants and blew a stray strand of hair from my face. Most of this week had passed in a busy blur. Sam and I continued to work with Victoria and Millie. I was confident the girls knew what they were doing and, with the help of Gladys, could manage the bakery Saturday and Sunday while we were gone. Gladys did need to leave early quite often, and she asked if she could continue to let the girls close up over the weekend. When pressed, she simply mentioned more cooking to do and left it at that.

"Let's go over the menu," Sam pulled out a chair and sat down. I joined her at the round table. It wasn't quite time to open yet, still a little early in the morning.

"Okay, first up, assorted breakfast pastries." I pulled out a notepad from my apron pocket and tucked a loose hair behind my ear.

"Scones!" Sam started enthusiastically listing items one by one. "Blueberry Scones, Dark Chocolate Chip and Walnut Scones, Honey Scones…"

"Do you think we should do a Walnut Butterscotch Drizzle Scone?"

"Definitely. Those crescents were to die for—a scone is bound to be good, too."

"We should probably do some savory." I chewed on my pen. "Bacon Cheddar Scones?"

"Good idea." Sam nodded. "Sausage, Feta, and Spinach Scones."

"What is next after scones?"

"How about tarts?"

"Yum. We could do several tarts made with cream cheese and fruits like blueberries, strawberries, raspberries, maybe even pineapple."

"What about the Donut Hole Clusters?"

"Yes, those are a must! Let me think…oh, I've got it! Personal Pancakes."

"What are those?" Sam tilted her head to the side.

"A stack of two or three pancakes that are small but made-to-order fresh," I told her. "We can put anything they want in the pancakes—oats, chocolate chips, blueberries, sprinkles, nuts, whatever we have on hand."

"I love it!" Sam smiled. "And now I want you to make pancakes for me tomorrow, too."

"Breakfast is covered then. Now, on to snacks and dessert."

"Cookies."

I hung my head. "We are going to have to be more specific than that, Sam," I said sarcastically as I looked back up at her.

She grinned and shrugged. "Lots of cookies."

"Geez, thanks." I rolled my eyes. "Fine, I'll start. Triple Chocolate Cookies, Pecan Pie Cookies, Peanut Butter Cookies."

"Okay, okay. Big Butterscotch Cookies, Butterscotch Oatmeal Cookies."

I scribbled hastily, trying to get them all written down as we continued. "Goodness, I hope I can read this when we are through. Monster Cookies, Walnut Dark Chocolate Cookies…surely that is enough?"

We added several pies to the list, including a Watermelon Pie, before deciding the time had come to open the café for the day.

"Do you think we need to buy the ingredients today?"

"The woman I spoke to said that the kitchen should be stocked with the basics," Sam said thoughtfully. "Why don't we take some fruit that Victoria won't be needing for the bakery and then make a list of what else to buy after we get there this evening?"

"That works for me." I flipped the sign on the door to open and went to the display case to find a scone for Flo. "I can't remember if Flo asked for a particular flavor. What do you think?"

"Take her a blueberry one. Blueberries boost brain power, who knows, maybe it will give her some extra-creative ideas for flower arrangements today."

I delivered the Blueberry Scone to Flo and bumped into Gladys as I returned to the bakery. "Good morning," I greeted her as we entered.

"Good morning, Piper. Shouldn't you girls be packing for your trip?" she asked me with a pat on my arm.

"Probably," I admitted. "We wanted to help Victoria and Millie open one last time though and see if they had any questions."

"You don't know how to take a break is more like it." Gladys shook her head.

I resisted the urge to stick my tongue out; I wasn't sure Gladys would put up with the rude gesture as much as Sam did.

"Sam, Gladys is kicking us out," I joked when we joined her at the counter.

"What? Why? When? From here?" She bobbed her head between the two of us, waiting for the punchline.

"Yes, from here, right now. She says we need to go get ready for the job this weekend. Really," I added in a mock whisper, "I think she's just ready to start the taste-testing and needs us out of the way."

"Can't say I blame her." Sam laughed. "Okay, Gladys," she came around and gave her a hug, "we will get out of your hair. Please, call us if you or the girls have any problems."

"Yes, we really appreciate you babysitting the bakery, but please don't hesitate to let us know if you need anything," I agreed.

"Shoo. Get on with you two, we'll be just fine," Gladys said, flapping her arms at us.

I sure hope everything goes well, I thought after telling Victoria and Millie bye and heading out the kitchen door to the parking lot in the back. "I'll pick you up in about an hour and a half?" I asked

Sam, double-checking the arrangements we had made.

"Yes. I'll see you then." She nodded as she slid into her yellow Juke.

I climbed up in my truck and smiled at the engine's growl when I cranked it. When I first learned to drive as a teenager, my parents insisted on putting me in a truck and not some small vehicle. As a doctor and nurse at the time, they had seen too many car accident victims and felt that I had a better chance of coming out of any fender bender or mild wreck unharmed if I were driving a larger vehicle. I had argued fiercely against it. Doctors' kids on tv drove convertibles and sports cars. *"It's so unfair,"* I had insisted. The joke was on me. I was hooked from the moment I stepped up into the cab. I felt big, important, powerful. Driving, I sat above half the other cars on the road. People got out of my way. I loved it and have never driven anything but a truck since.

I pulled up at my apartment complex a scant six minutes later. I needed to pack and look up directions to Lion's Cove, specifically The Cove's Cabins at Lion's Cove where the wellness retreat would be held. Inside my cozy one-bedroom apartment, I dropped my keys into the bowl on the side table in the foyer and made a beeline to the kitchen for a glass of water. And groaned. The kitchen was a mess. I left in such a hurry this morning that I didn't clean up the dishes from breakfast.

Grabbing the glass bowl off the counter, I attempted to use the spray nozzle to loosen the dried bits of butterscotch now hardened to the sides. Crumpling the parchment paper up as I snatched it from the sheet pan, I tossed it at the trash…and missed. Sigh. I picked it up and threw it away. *Dishwasher running, check,* I mentally congratulated myself as I walked from the kitchen to my bedroom. *Closet, here I come.*

Relieved that I didn't need to fret quite so much over outfits for this trip (choosing outfits for the spa had been foreign territory for me), I grabbed two pairs of cargo pants. I chose a heather gray and a teal t-shirt with the Ooey-Gooey Goodness logo, the bakery's name stamped over a broken cookie dripping with fat chocolate chips. I folded the shirts into small squares to toss in my duffle.

Before I got to the other necessities, my cell phone rang. I could barely hear it from the entry where I had left it. Sprinting to the front of my apartment—thank goodness it was small—I hit answer on the last ring.

"Hello," I said.

Static crackled through the line.

"Hello? Hello?" I tried again.

"Piper…me…is Landon…" The voice cut in and out as the static continued. "…see you…line…weekend."

"Landon, what? I can't hear you."

"Piper? Pi…?"

"Landon? Are you there?" The silence continued. I hung up the phone. "Well, that was odd," I spoke aloud. Tapping the yellow button for my call log, I hit recent and tapped the number on the screen. Saving the new number as Landon in my address book, I slipped the phone in my pocket, keeping it close in case he called again.

It took no time at all to finish packing pajamas, underwear, toiletries, extra socks, and so on. Zipping my bag closed, I took one more look around the room. Satisfied I hadn't forgotten anything, I slung the bag over my shoulder, set the thermostat so it wouldn't kick on so often over the next couple of days, fished my keys out of the bowl, and locked up.

Chapter 9

The drive to pick up Sam passed pleasantly. I rolled the windows down and shut off the radio, simply enjoying the salty breeze playing with my hair and listening to the waves lap the shore. Unlike my apartment close to town, Sam lived in a duplex right on the beach. Sometimes I wanted to find my own place near the water, but it wasn't in my budget right now. *Besides,* I grinned to myself as I pulled into the second spot of the garage on Sam's side, *it's not like I don't spend the majority of my weekends here for free anyway, why pay rent on an expensive place?*

I noticed the garage door for the other half of the duplex was shut tight. Griff must still be away on business. The duplex, weathered and sporting a chipped baby blue siding, had been a gift to Griff and Sam when their father got elected mayor. Deidra insisted that she and Gregory could no longer live in this "quaint starter home" if they wanted to be taken seriously as leaders of the town. Gregory Lowe had purchased the entire duplex outright and given it to Griff as a college graduation present, on the conditions that Sam would be given the other half of the living space and it would not be rented out to anyone else. I had been surprised either Griff or Sam had accepted the home as a gift.

"Well, Griff saw it as a blessing," Sam told me once when I asked her about it. "He says this way he is able to save up more for a home and family in the future. I wasn't crazy about it at first, but it makes it easier to pour money into the bakery and still put a good portion aside, too. Plus, I love being near the ocean. How could I say no to that?"

Now, as I walked up the eight wooden steps to knock on Sam's door, I was definitely glad for the gift house. I considered it my home away from home, besides the bakery, of course.

By the time I reached the top step, Sam had the door open. "I heard you pull up," she greeted. "Did you google the directions?"

"Yes, it will take about three and a half hours to get there."

"Wow, Lion's Cove is further away than I thought."

"Yeah. We still have some time though. I think if we leave by eleven that will be plenty of time to find the kitchen, take stock of things, and buy any supplies or ingredients that we need tonight."

"I was hoping you would say that," Sam confessed as we made the way into the kitchen.

"Why's that?" I asked curiously.

"Because I'm starving and I still haven't packed; I accidentally fell asleep," she admitted. "I was hoping you would make your amazing Spinach and Artichoke Grilled Cheese? Please?" She blinked up at me like a kid with puppy dog eyes.

"Fine." I laughed, swatting at her. "Go pack and I'll make us an early lunch."

"That is why you're my best friend." Sam smiled.

I shook my head as she nearly skipped, or at least the closest I've seen for a grown woman skipping. My stomach growled. *Okay, okay. I agree the sandwich sounds good, geez*, I thought to my rumbling insides.

"Griff must still be out of town," I commented as we took our plates out onto the back verandah of the duplex, overlooking blinding sands and gorgeous blue water. Sleek, blue-gray fish shot like torpedoes into the air from the cresting waves. Sam cringed as a seagull succeeded in snatching one from midair. She hated seeing animals get hurt, any kind.

"Did you limit yourself to only three or four pantsuits for our two-day trip?" I teased to distract her. "Oomph!" I rubbed my temple where she threw a piece of crust at me. That earned us the attention of a few nearby seagulls.

"Now look what you've done, Piper." Sam gave an exaggerated eye roll.

"Me? You're going to blame this on me?" A particularly bold seagull winged between our deck chairs. I leaned out of the way.

"Of course, it is absolutely your fault, and for the record, I packed regular clothes."

"What do you mean regular clothes? You wear slacks all the time."

"I packed jeans and t-shirts."

"T-shirts?" I narrowed my eyes.

Sam finally ducked my gaze. "Fine. Maybe they are cute t-shirts, but they still count as t-shirts."

"Ha!"

We finished our sandwiches, delicious and creamy spinach dip oozing from between buttered and crisp-toasted bread. I tossed the paper plates in the trash and cleaned the counter while Sam did the dishes.

"You ready?" she asked a few minutes later.

"Yep, let's get out of here." I gave her a thumbs-up.

"Road trip!" She clapped and danced in place, making me laugh.

"Get in the truck," I told her, shaking my head. "We still have to stop for gas."

Piling Sam's belongings in the back seat beside my own, I backed out and waited for her to close the garage before taking off down the coastal road. We wound our way along Beachside Drive for several miles before I turned back inland. I pulled into the first gas station I saw and hopped out to fill the tank.

"I'm going to the restroom," Sam called as she exited the passenger side.

I spent a few minutes people watching while gas chugged into the 26-gallon tank of my truck. *Yikes.* I cringed as I caught sight of the dollars and cents rolling higher and higher. *Definitely better to people watch; paying for gas is painful,* I decided to myself.

My eyes roamed the parking lot, watching as a toddler dropped her Skittles and commenced screaming at the top of her lungs, the teenagers at the next pump made out in the car even though their gas pump had stopped long ago, and a young boy helped his grandmother sit down in the car, showing her patience and care. Having run out of people at the gas station to view, my eyes landed in the parking lot next door. It was a seafood and burger joint, and the parking lot contained only a handful of vehicles.

"I got you a Snickers." Sam appeared out of nowhere at my elbow, making me jump.

"You nearly gave me a heart attack," I griped at her but took the candy anyway.

"Yeah, you were pretty zoned out. What are you staring at?"

"I'm not staring; I'm people watching. You see that girl in the parking lot, over at the seafood place?" I waited for Sam to nod before I continued, "She nearly broke her ankle in a pothole with those heels. She looked like a baby giraffe learning to walk!"

"You're so mean."

"Then there was a guy whose hat blew away before that. Look, someone else is coming out of the restaurant."

Sam leaned forward a bit. "Is that…?"

"Griff?" I asked her. "Maybe this town is where he came for his business trip. Wait, are we even out of Seashell Bay yet?" Seashell Bay was the picturesque little town we lived in; I knew we had been driving a while but wasn't sure where the city limits technically ended.

"Nope. I'm going to call him." She pulled her phone from her pocket.

"No! Don't." I grabbed her arm and pointed back to the neighboring parking lot. Griff now held the door open for a tall woman wearing a tight yellow dress. She grabbed his arm, and I watched as Griff escorted her toward his silver truck. *How did I miss that truck?* I chastised myself. Suddenly Griff stopped and reached to his side, unclipping his phone.

"Crap," Sam mumbled beside me. She had hit send after all. I listened to her side of the conversation. "Hey. Yeah. No, I didn't need anything. Where are you? Oh, still at work—I see. Okay. Okay, love you too. Bye."

Sam put the phone back in her pocket and shook her head. We watched as Griff helped the woman into his passenger seat, got in, and drove away.

"Working out of town? He said he was still at work?" I asked Sam. I didn't know how to process what I had seen.

Click.

Sam and I both startled as the gas pump shut off with a last shudder.

"Piper, I'm sorry. I...I don't know. I'll find out more from him, maybe she's a client."

"Whom he took to dinner," I said as I placed the nozzle back on the pump with a bang.

"Yeah..."

"And who was very dressed up."

"Well..." Sam shrugged. "We will get to the bottom of this. I know Griff wouldn't have said he had feelings for you if he were seeing someone."

"Then why did he lie to you about work?"

"He...I don't know," she admitted, "but I'm sure there's a reason."

"Let's just go," I told her. We climbed into the truck. I tossed the Snickers bar into the console. As if by magic, my appetite had vanished.

Merging back onto the highway, I tried to shake the unsettling feelings that snaked their way through me similar to how the road snaked along the coast, back and forth, back and forth. It really didn't matter that Griff took a woman, a beautiful woman, out to lunch. It hurt like hell, but it didn't matter.

And it shouldn't hurt either, for that matter. I hadn't even begun to unravel the tangled emotions and raw nerves that sparked against each other after my ordeal with first Abigail and then Griff's unexpected revelation. Throw Landon and his unexpected appearance and unknown intentions into the mix, and I was just plain finished with drama and intrigue in my life. *I'm much better suited to cookies*, I thought. *Cookies make sense, ingredients can be measured, the desired outcome achieved, no problem. Usually.*

"Piper!"

Sam's screech at last penetrated the fog of confusion clouding my brain. I glanced over and was shocked to see she was white-knuckling the armrest on the door.

"Piper, the road!" she yelled, pointing.

I whipped my gaze forward and saw through the windshield a large eighteen-wheeler bearing down on me. Directly on me. Alarm bells sounded in my head. *I'm in the wrong lane!* I tapped the brakes and wrenched the steering wheel right. Angry bursts of a horn sounded from the truck as, seconds later, it roared past. Sam sat silently, staring at me from the passenger seat. I slowed and eased over to the shoulder of the road.

I closed my eyes and released a shuddering breath. My best friend squeezed my hand.

"I'm so, so sorry." I looked at Sam. "I don't even know what to say. I was in my own head and didn't even realize I stopped paying attention. I'm sorry." It wasn't adequate, not nearly enough. I could have gotten us both killed, and I knew it.

"I think I should drive," Sam spoke firmly, but with kindness. She squeezed my hand again, and her eyes were filled with compassion where I deserved to see anger. She held out her hand. I nodded and dropped the keys into it.

Chapter 10

"Wow!" I said as I spun in another circle. "This kitchen is huge."

"Not at all what I expected in a remote cabin," Sam agreed.

I looked at my watch. Four fifteen p.m. We had arrived in Lion's Cove only half an hour ago. The trip had taken much longer than planned, first because a wreck shut down traffic for over forty minutes. After that, Sam ended up stopping to ask directions to The Cove's Cabins because the navigation we were using on my phone kept sending us in circles. Her phone died, and the charger sat tucked away in a suitcase somewhere. It turned out this cabin resort area was less than six months old. No surprise that the directions hadn't been perfect considering that I don't run my phone updates every time it prompts me to.

"I'll leave you ladies to it," said Roy, the maintenance man who had been tasked with our grand tour and handing over the keys to the cabin we would bunk in as well as keys to the cabin designated for dining.

"Thank you, Roy." I smiled. He nodded and left. I heard the soft sound of his golf cart as he puttered off, on to his next chore, I was sure.

"Okay, let's check the list," Sam said, all business.

No further discussion of the incident on the road had come up. Sam had simply parked the truck, handed me my keys back, and given me a big hug when we arrived at the main office. The liaison for Breaking Chains hadn't arrived yet, which is how Roy ended up being our tour guide. A good sport about it, Roy had handed us up into his golf cart as if we were royalty and driven us through the dunes to see the many colorful cabins. He loved his job here, he told us, and took great pride in maintaining the cabins and keeping the beach sprawled before them clean as could be.

I unfolded the small sheets of paper from my pocket and flattened them onto the counter.

"Flour," I read off first.

"Flour," Sam said as she swung each cabinet door wide open and left them that way. "Got it, ten pounds of flour," she said at last.

"Sugar."

"Sugar…yep, there's a three-pound bag of that."

"Eggs?"

"Eggs, yes, but only a dozen." Sam frowned from the refrigerator.

"We will definitely need more than that." I peeled a clean piece of paper from the back of the small stack and wrote out a new list. TO BUY, I wrote in large letters at the top. *Eggs.* I thought about our many recipes. *Probably at least three more dozen.*

After another forty-five minutes, going from list to list and cabinet to cabinet, we had a fairly long grocery list compiled.

"Do we buy groceries now or make some test cookies first?" Sam asked.

"Let's go ahead and make at least two batches. We need to see if the oven works, check the microwave for melting, see what the measuring cup and mixing bowl situation looks like; basically, let's cook something so we know if we have everything to cook with. I'd hate to drive all the way to town to get ingredients then come back and find out we need four other things to bake efficiently."

~

"Phew!" I wiped droplets of sweat from my forehead. "What time is it, Sam?" I asked as I scrubbed the last dish and placed it in the rack to dry.

"Almost seven," she answered with a glance at her watch as she paused mid-sweep and then continued to tidy up the floors.

"No wonder I'm hungry. I didn't plan on waiting this long before we went back to town for ingredients and supplies." We had ended up getting the dough ready for the scones along with baking more cookies than planned.

"Let's go. We have enough done for tonight. Pancakes won't take long in the morning, and we don't need to prep for them tonight."

I nodded, wiping down the last drops of water from the counter and drying my hands. A scan of the large kitchen showed Sam to be right—there was nothing left for us to do tonight.

"Maybe we can find a good place for supper in Lion's Cove," I said. "Those test cookies were good, but I need something with a little more sustenance." *Like a whole bushel of fried shrimp.* I imagined the crisp, golden, buttery shrimp and licked my lips. "Seafood?"

"Sure, that sounds fantastic." Sam nodded.

It took us half an hour to maneuver all of the tiny blacktop roads back into Lion's Cove.

"I don't know why they are even called 'The Cove's Cabins.'" Sam rolled her eyes. "It doesn't feel like they are near the city of Lion's Cove itself."

"True, but it is the closest town around," I pointed out.

Our supper at The Shrimper, a small, weathered building with wood siding and shrimp crates lining the porch rails, was delicious. I ordered the Big Shrimp Basket; Sam enjoyed the Crab-Stuffed Ravioli. The portions were enormous and the food absolute perfection. Or maybe those grilled cheese sandwiches were just a long time ago; either way, we both cleaned our plates with gusto. Even though we skipped dessert at the restaurant, opting for the bag of cookies in the truck, by the time we left, it was dark out.

"I guess Lion's Cove isn't as big as I thought it was," I said after getting in the truck and scrolling through my phone.

"Why do you say that?" Sam asked as she buckled her seatbelt.

"Google says there isn't a Walmart within an hour of here."

"I think I saw a Grocer Giant a few blocks down the road. I don't know if they have more than food, but we can check it out."

The Grocer Giant had only groceries. We were able to find all of the ingredients but none of the supplies.

"We still need a large whisk and a second set of measuring cups, plus a powdered sugar shaker and a glass measuring cup for melting things in," I read the items off the list before tossing it back into the console.

"It looks like," Sam leaned closer to her glowing phone screen, "there's a Dollar Store that is still open for the next thirty minutes. It's about a ten-minute drive on the other side of town, I think."

Sam passed me her phone, and I glanced at the directions. Neither of us saw any promising stores closer to us; evidently, Lion's Cove rolled up the sidewalks early.

"Dollar Store it is," I said, throwing the gearshift into drive. "You can tell me how to get there." So, with Sam reading the directions, off we went.

Streets deteriorated as we drove. I watched out the window as old but clean buildings gave way to graffiti-covered walls and garbage littered alleys. Women with long legs and short skirts smoked on a corner. Soon, only every other street light remained lit. The others sported busted or missing bulbs. Darkness edged closer, making the already smaller side-streets seem narrower.

We made it to the other side of town in about eight minutes. I found myself hoping we would make it out even more quickly than that.

"I think we might be in a bad neighborhood," Sam said as she studied the dimly lit parking lot, the beer bottles littering the empty grass lot to the left and the large graffiti drawing of a middle finger decorated the side of the Dollar Store building. Sam had been focused on the phone and directions and hadn't seen just how rough this part of town had gotten.

"Well, we're here now. Let's just go in, grab the stuff, and get out." I felt for the pocket knife clipped to my pants, making sure it was within reach. For what, I don't know and hoped I didn't have to find out; still, it made me feel better as I got out of the truck and walked with Sam through the dimly lit parking lot.

"No splitting up," Sam warned as we entered the store.

The store was old. I mean wood floors old. Not nice ones, but splintered and stained wood that rolled up and down through the store, warped from age and nowhere near level anymore. I wondered if it ever had been. Most of the aisles were labeled with signs hung from the ceiling, though several hung by only one end and you had to tilt your head sideways to read the words.

The kitchen aisle, miraculously beneath a sign that still gripped the ceiling by cables on both ends, was located at the front of the store. Sam picked out a whisk, doing her best to find the sturdiest option, while I gathered up plastic and glass measuring cups.

"They don't have the powdered sugar shaker," Sam said as we made a third pass down the aisle, checking into the recesses of the shelves.

"It's fine. We can make do," I said. Punch a few holes in a paper plate – voila – homemade sugar shaker. We carried our purchases to the counter where a redhead reclined against the large case holding cigarettes, chomping on a piece of gum like a cow on cud. It was not attractive, but I wasn't about to tell her. A nose ring glinted in the fluorescent light and I blinked, *was that a puppy she wore on her nose?*

"Hey!" she barked. Sam took a step back and I pulled my eyes away from the metal dog decorating her left nostril.

"Hi," I said. "Just these, please" I sat all of the measuring cups down and grabbed the whisk from Sam to add to the pile.

"What are you two doing in this neighborhood? You lost?" she asked, not even looking down as she scanned the purchases but narrowing her eyes and staring at us.

"Nope, not lost," Sam said.

"We didn't find any other open stores in Lion's Cove," I admitted.

"You should've gone far away then," she said. "Don't you know pretty girls get grabbed out here?"

"You're out here," I replied, not sure what to make of her. Was the woman issuing a threat or a warning? The scowl on her face in between bubble gum chews hadn't changed.

"But I've always been here," she said as if that should clear it up for me. "Twelve dollars," she said before I could think of anything else. The second I handed over the money she tipped her head at the door. "Get back where you came from before you get hurt."

I won't lie – Sam and I basically sprinted to the truck. I punched the lock and we sat for a moment trying to catch our breath.

"Okay, I'm ready to get out of here," Sam said buckling her seatbelt.

"That makes two of us," I agreed. I cranked the truck and put it in reverse, moving to back out of the parking spot.

"Piper, look!" Sam tapped my arm as she said it, causing me to slam on the breaks.

"What?" I asked darting glances all around, images of gangs or the redheaded woman or a drunken hobo all assaulting me at once. "What am I looking for?" I asked after seconds passed and nothing terrible had jumped out to get me.

"I think that's Landon," Sam pointed to a man with his back to us at the doorway of a business two doors down from the Dollar Store.

"I can't tell," I leaned forward in my seat. The door opened before him and the dim, yellow light that spilled out shone on the sandy-colored hair. I still wasn't certain. "Why would Landon be out here?" I asked.

"You're right, I just thought it looked like him. You don't forget a hottie like that," Sam sighed and I rolled my eyes.

The man at the door turned then, looking over his shoulder down the street to both sides. Before he ducked his head lower and stepped into the building, we saw his face.

"It was him!" Sam said. "How strange. What is that place anyway?"

"One way to find out," I told her. I backed out of the parking spot and drove slowly down the street. Drawing close to the building I peered at the sign in the window.

"Thai Massage," Sam read the sign aloud.

"Yeah, but the sign isn't lit and the door says 'closed' on it," I shook my head. "What in the world would Landon...." I broke off as bits and pieces of information from Breaking Chains pamphlets flitted to the forefront of my mind. The closed sign. The ATM at the corner of the building. The out-of-the-way location.

"Piper, you don't think…did Landon just go into a brothel?" Sam looked at me, wide eyes mirroring my own crazy thoughts.

"I don't know," I said while eyeballing my rearview mirror. "Right now, it doesn't matter. If we don't get out of here, we are going to have company."

Sam turned in her seat and saw what I was seeing: two men stumbling out of an alley on the opposite side of the road. Both had shaved heads and tattoos running up their arms. That wasn't what made Samantha gulp or had me speeding back toward a well-lit part of town. Nope, that had nothing to do with the tough-guy look and everything to do with the butt of a pistol we could see sticking out of the front of the pants of one and the beers they were both chugging like water. The time had come for us to leave.

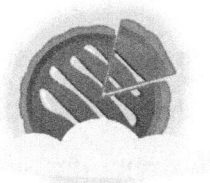

Chapter 11

Landon looked over his shoulder one last time before dismissing the feeling of being watched.

"Hey Sugar," the voice said, small and sweet as honey, as the door in front of him opened and drew his attention. The tiny, dark-haired woman reached out one hand and tugged at his shirt, a long pink fingernail raking his chest along the way. "Come on in," she winked, "you look like you need to relax."

"Actually," Landon spoke low. "I was hoping we could talk?"

The woman opened the door wide and smoke drifted out as Landon entered.

"Follow me, Sugar. Coco knows just what you need," she said. Turning with a flourish, she sashayed down the hall in her tall gold stilettos and pink mini-dress never doubting for a moment that the new guy would be right behind her. As she walked, she closed her eyes with a grimace, not realizing the mirrors lining the hall gave the man behind her a clear picture of what she thought about the night ahead of her.

A short time later, Landon slipped back into the dark parking lot. He glanced around. A few extra cars were in the lot, and two drunk guys walking down the street laughed and shoved each other. He didn't see anything out of the ordinary, no reason for the odd sensation making the hair stand up on the back of his neck. He slid into the driver's seat of a beat-up sedan and drove away. A final glance in his mirror revealed a flick of the blinds in the front room of the massage parlor he'd just left.

Chapter 12

Sam and I slept as good as can be expected in a strange place and after a big dose of adrenaline in the rough part of town. In other words, we barely slept at all. With no regard to our need for rest, the alarm sounded at four in the morning.

Beep.

I groaned. *Didn't I shut off the alarm?* I thought as I groped for my phone on the floor beside my bunk. Thank goodness Sam and I were the only two sharing this little cabin. It had two sets of bunk beds which meant we were both able to have a bottom bunk. Little else inhabited the small space. No baseboards or trim had been installed; I got the feeling we were tucked away in an unfinished unit. I didn't mind. It made sense that the members of the wellness retreat should be in the vacation-ready cabins.

Beep. Beep.

A text? At this time of day that couldn't be a good sign. I snatched up the phone and swiped my finger across the screen.

Sam got up and walked to the small bathroom with half shower, toilet, and sink as I read the message. And groaned again.

"What's with you this morning?" Sam asked. "You sound like my grandma and her arthritis with all that moaning and groaning. Who's that?" she asked the last question pointing her toothbrush at my phone.

"Gladys," I said.

"Ohmygosh!" Sam threw her hands up and yelped around the toothbrush now in her mouth. "Did the bakery burn down? Did the girls not show up? Did Millie flood the dishwasher?" Toothpaste dripped down her chin as she spewed out all of her questions at once.

"Gladys," I said again, standing up out of bed and stretching, "texted me to say Griff is already in the bakery parking lot this morning. He wanted to talk to me."

"Oh. Okay," Sam went back in the bathroom to rinse her mouth and wash her face.

I waited. Sure enough, it didn't take long.

"Hey!" she popped her head back into the main room. "Why in the world is Griff at the bakery at four a.m.? Why didn't he text you?"

"I might have temporarily blocked his number after *the incident* yesterday," I said using air quotes.

Sam stared for a millisecond and then laughed. "Of course. I should have known."

"This weekend I'm just going to concentrate on baking and encouraging these amazing people who are here for a well-earned retreat."

"Fine," Sam shrugged. "I'm done in here, your turn."

By five-thirty, we had all of the scones baked and lined up on a short buffet table. I finished mixing the pancake batter and separated it into five medium mixing bowls. That would make it easier to add in items and be able to do many flavored pancakes at once, without having to make new batter for every time someone ordered a different flavor. Sam had just finished placing the last blueberry on one of two beautiful fresh fruit tarts.

The kitchen only took up half of the Dining cabin. The other half was one large room decorated with Southern Cattails, starfish, and driftwood. Even the tables themselves were constructed from massive driftwood pieces and weathered tree trunks that were fit together to create individual pieces of art. Each table was topped with a slab of glass, to protect the wood and provide a flat surface for eating while maintaining the natural beauty of the structure. The walls of the room were painted a natural, light sand color, the perfect backdrop to give the understated décor the spotlight.

Two big cased openings, similar to the windows for a concession stand at a ballpark, allowed sounds to filter through to the kitchen. One opening had a wide sill. On it sat stacks of light blue plates and cups of plastic silverware.

Tap. Tap. Tap.

Sam and I turned at the sound of light tapping to find three people standing at the serving window.

"Good morning," the man in the front waved. "I hope we aren't too early."

"Not at all," Sam smiled and stepped to the opening. We had already decided she, being the more personable of us both, would take orders and I would handle the pancake griddle. "I need just one moment to get these tarts situated on the buffet, but you can pick out your Personal Pancake Platter flavors in the meantime." She placed a small chalkboard sign on the sill and hurried out of the kitchen with the Blueberry Banana Tart and the Strawberry Kiwi Tart balancing in her hands.

"What can I get for you?" Sam returned in seconds.

"I'll have the Dark Chocolate Chip Pancakes," the second person in line, a tall woman with hair in a severe bun, piped up.

"Can't resist chocolate can you, Regina?" the man in front of her teased. "Blueberry for me," he ordered.

"A plain pancake please," the last in line, a short, round man with a jolly face smiled.

Expecting many more Blueberry Pancake orders for the day, I dumped a carton of blueberries into one mixing bowl and stirred. After ladling six of those onto the griddle, I made a few more pancake circles, this time tossing the dark chocolate chips in after. I wouldn't add them to an entire bowl of batter just yet; I knew not everyone enjoyed dark chocolate's bitter notes.

Sam passed platters of pancakes through the opening as I handed them to her. "Don't forget your fork," she said, holding the cup of silverware toward the happy breakfasters.

"Maybe we should have put silverware on the table," I said.

"I'm just glad this place had silverware," Sam said. "I never would have thought to buy any; our usual cookies and pastries don't require any."

The breakfast crowd came in clusters, most likely groups that had bunked in the same cabin or friends who decided the night before to meet up for breakfast. There were very few lulls. It seemed from conversations we overheard that the wellness retreat would be a combination of relaxing activities, reflection, and team building skills

"Sam," I called after a few minutes of inactivity, "do you think I need to make more batter or is that about it for people?"

"How much do you have left?" she asked leaning through the opening to look to the door.

I scraped the side of the bowl to get the last of the milk chocolate chip batter out and surveyed the others before answering. "Probably enough for four or five pancakes, provided they don't choose sprinkles or dark chocolate as flavors."

Sam let out a gasp and I looked to see her staring toward the entrance.

"Don't tell me, twenty more appetites just walked in?" I guessed.

"No. Just one. I don't know what kind of appetite he has though," she mumbled, stepping away from the window.

"What do you mean?" My forehead crinkled in confusion.

"Good morning!" a voice exclaimed. "Piper, Sam, how are you? Something smells delicious and I'm starved."

I stared as Landon walked up, hands in his pockets, with wind-tousled hair and a big smile.

Another surprise appearance? *What is he doing here?* I wondered.

Finally, I found words. "Good morning," I returned. "You can have the last stack of Chocolate Chip Pancakes," I told him as I flipped one over on the griddle.

"I must be one lucky man," he grinned.

"Why are you here?" I couldn't resist asking. It just seemed too strange.

"What do you mean? I called you earlier and told you I got reassigned and would see you this weekend, remember?"

The garbled staticky phone call! "We had a horrible connection. I didn't hear anything you said." I explained to Landon.

Just then, a voice in the dining hall called out for Landon.

"Sorry, gotta go," he said.

I stared at the plate of pancakes and shook my head – having my friend Landon back in my life might be more frustrating than fun.

Landon pulled his hands free to hug a few people that he seemed to know and I saw a small black object fall from his pocket. I waited for him to notice, to pick it up, but when he didn't, I handed the spatula to Sam and walked into the main dining room.

Before I took more than a few steps, the little round man from the first line this morning clapped his hands for attention at the front of the dining area. Everyone quieted.

"Let us bow in prayer and ask the Lord's blessing and restoration for our weekend before we begin our recreation activities," he said.

I bowed and stood still, along with everyone else. I listened as he prayed for rest, for peace in knowing they were bringing help daily to victims of human trafficking, and for wisdom to get many out safely.

"Now, Father," he prayed, "help this weekend bring refreshment and closer bonds to each of our teammates and keep us safe during all of our activities. Thank you for this beautiful, peaceful place to enjoy your creation. Amen."

"Amen," voices echoed.

Everyone that was finished eating stood to leave and the crowd surged toward the door. I was forced to back up out of the way until they passed. The room emptied faster than I would have expected and Landon was not among the stragglers. I peered around the floor in the last spot I'd seen him. Sure enough, after a moment I found a small black object wedged against a table leg. Picking it up I was surprised to discover it was a tube of lipstick.

"I guess we need to clean up this mess?" Sam asked, gesturing to the plates and cups stacked all over the tables as she joined me. "What do you have there?"

"Landon dropped something out of his pocket. I swear he was in this area, but the only thing I've found is this lipstick."

"That doesn't make sense. What's that sticker on the side?"

"A 1-800 number…"

"Oh."

"Yeah. I don't know what to think about any of this. Why is he here? Why would he go in that massage parlor so late last night? Is that where the lipstick came from?" I shook my head. Too many questions, too few answers.

Sam's phone rang just then and I shoved the lipstick into the side pocket of my cargo pants. Sam looked at the screen and lifted it to show me, raising her eyebrows. The caller idea said Griff.

"Don't tell me," I said.

"Yep. My brother's been texting me asking why you aren't answering him. Now he's calling.

You really should talk to him, Piper. That's the only way to figure things out."

"I know. I will." I plucked up several dishes to haul to the sink.

"When?" she pushed.

"When I have time," I hedged.

The door opened from outside and Roy stuck his head inside.

"Hey, Roy," I waved. "Did you want some leftover pancakes or scones?"

"Well, I don't reckon I know what a scone is. Pancakes sound mighty fine, though." He nodded. "I came to tell you girls not to worry about cleaning up. My wife is the caretaker and will be in shortly with a few girls to clean before the company bringing in lunch gets here."

"Thanks, Roy," I said. "I'll get you a box of pancakes if you'll give me just a second."

I heard the door again as I plopped pancakes into a carry-out container.

"Hi, Sam," I heard Landon say before I saw him. "Hey, Piper. Sorry I didn't get to eat those pancakes. I came in to tell you that we could use another player for volleyball; we're one short."

"I'll go," Sam spoke up and I looked at her in surprise. She met my eyes and continued, "Piper just told me she had to go make a very important phone call, otherwise I'm sure she would have loved to play."

I shot her a dirty look. She knew full well I didn't want to call Griff, yet here she was making sure I had privacy and free time to make it happen.

"Great," Landon said. "Let's go before they start without us."

"Here you go, Roy." He thanked me for the pancakes and returned to his golf cart.

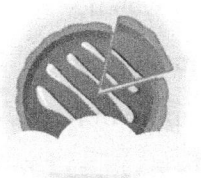

Chapter 13

I walked down the cabin steps and stopped. The Dining cabin stood in the center of the many smaller guest cabins. The cabin Sam and I bunked in couldn't even be seen from here; it sat furthest from the ocean. I didn't really want to go all the way back there to call Griff. I meandered down the trails between cabins to the shoreline. A rowdy volleyball game could be seen in the sand a few yards to my left. To the right, other than a smattering of people in lounge chairs, the beach exuded quiet and calm. I turned to the right.

What am I going to say to Griff? What about the woman he took to lunch?

Dropping down to sit, far away from the few people on this stretch of sand, I hugged my knees and watched the waves. In. Out. Roaring up. Crashing down. I watched as the breathtaking display mimicked my thoughts, my hopes. For a place where I found such peace, the ocean definitely displayed chaos of its own.

Pulling my phone from my pants pocket, I unblocked Griff's number. Message notifications starting popping up like popcorn. I scrolled to the top of the list. Eight from Griff. Two from my mother. One from Gladys.

I opened the one from Gladys first and read the single line,

Gladys: Don't worry, everything is fine.

Great. I hadn't been worried, now I wondered if I should be.

Next came mom's messages.

Mom: Got your message. Have fun on catering job. Love you.

Mom: Don't get kidnapped.

Ha, hilarious Mom, I thought, rolling my eyes. I would text her back later. Now on to Griff. I took a deep breath.

Griff: Piper, I'm sorry I had to go out of town. I still want to talk.

Griff: Can we do dinner?

Griff: I really hope we can talk. Are you mad at me?

Griff: Gladys is at the bakery. Are you okay? Is Sam okay? Where are y'all?

Griff: I responded to the fire call at the bakery, don't worry – everything is fine.

Griff: Please call. I miss you.

My heart skipped a beat. *A fire!* That's it. I dialed and listened to the phone ring.

"Hello?"

"Gladys," I said, "What is going on, is everyone okay? There was a fire?"

"No. There was no fire," Gladys said. "I texted you and told you everything is fine. Who said anything about a fire?"

"Griff…" I tried to explain.

"Oh good! You're finally talking to that boy again. It's about time."

"No, I haven't spoken to him. He sent a text about a fire call at the bakery."

"Oh that, psh" Gladys said and I could picture her rolling her eyes. "Millie went and accidentally yanked that fire alarm with the broom handle, that's all."

"How in the world – you know what, never mind. So, you three and the Ooey Gooey are good?" I asked.

"Yes, better than good. It's been busier than church on Easter Sunday. Well, maybe not that busy but close. Victoria has been baking up a storm." Gladys paused. "Yes, everything is great. Especially after that hunky fireman came and assured us there was no fire. And once Millie mopped up all that water from the sprinklers. Once that little hiccup ended, everything has been fine and dandy."

My eyes widened at the thought of firemen and floodwaters in the Ooey Gooey. Relieved no real harm had been done, I still felt guilty just thinking about the work everyone must be putting in. I didn't know what I could do for Gladys, we would have to figure that out, but I bet Sam would agree with me to give Millie and Victoria a little bonus.

"Piper," Gladys broke through my thoughts, "you really should call Griff."

"Yeah, that's what Sam says. Y'all shouldn't gang up on a girl like that," I joked.

"I've got to run. More customers," Gladys said.

"Okay, bye." I hung up the phone, the screen reverting back to my message list. My thumb hovered over Griff's name. With a sigh, I tapped the green call button and waited for him to pick up.

"Piper," one word, a sigh.

"Hey," I said.

"Piper, I wanted to apologize for being an idiot when your friend Landon came by, and for not finishing our conversation."

"You had to leave for work, I understand."

"Listen, can we make plans for dinner? Maybe Sunday night?"

"I don't know what time we will wrap up here this weekend actually," I told him honestly. "Maybe, if we are back to Seashell Bay by then."

"Griffin!" a high-pitched voice broke through the background noise on Griff's side.

"What the…. Piper, I've got to go," Griff said.

"Griffin, Kendra and I have been looking everywhere for you," another voice spoke. This one I recognized. Deidra.

"Sorry, Piper. I'll explain later but I have to go. Bye." Griff hung up and I stared once more at the screen in front of me. I don't know how I expected the phone call to go, but I know that wasn't it. *Who the heck is Kendra?* A picture of the woman in the yellow dress flashed through my mind.

Laughter erupted from down the beach. The volleyball game appeared to be going strong, laughter and taunts flowing freely from both sides of the net. I watched the ball being served. WHAP! The sound traveled through the air as a girl opposite Sam struck it with all her might. A little bit of sport might be just what I needed to get my mind off of Griff. *Might as well see if they need another player to give someone a rest,* I decided.

"Piper!" Landon called out as I approached. "Perfect timing. Danny here just went down with a sprained ankle. You up to take his place?"

"I'll give it a shot," I told him. I took my place in the open corner and someone tossed me the ball to serve. I tossed the ball high. As I swung my arms up to serve it over the net, I released all of my frustration into the move. WHACK! I smiled with pleasure when the ball soared past the players in the back row and gave a satisfying THUNK into the sand inside the bounds.

"Whoop!" A few cheers and a whistle split the air. Energy picked up and we spent a good half hour hitting, diving, and laughing.

"Good game," both sides called out to each other when we finished. The side with me, Landon, and Sam ended up winning by only two points.

"We really need to get cleaned up and start prepping desserts for after lunch," Sam said as she wiped sweat from her forehead.

Equally sweaty, I nodded in agreement. Thanking everyone for letting us join, we began the short trek around all of the cabins to ours in the back.

"Did you call?" Sam asked.

"Yep," I said. Knowing curiosity ate at Sam, it was fun to make her work for the information. I kept walking, brushing my hands along some of the tall beach grasses growing along the path. I glanced up as a bird of some kind, not very large, glided overhead. I didn't even look at Sam, but I could feel her frustration mounting.

"And?" Sam pushed. "Did you talk to Griff?"

"I did."

"Piper…" she glared at me.

"I also spoke to Gladys."

"Fine, I'll bite," Sam rolled her eyes. "What did Gladys say?"

"She said that Millie accidentally tripped the fire alarm and that the bakery has been busier than church on Easter." I watched the information sink in as Sam tilted her head and thought about what I told her.

"So, Millie started a small fire?" she asked. I could hear the spray of gravel as she picked up her pace to get closer and hear me better.

"Nope," I answered. "Pulled the handle with the broom."

"How would she manage that?"

"I don't know. Honestly, I decided not to ask."

We had arrived at the cabin, our little home away from home. I took the steps two at a time. There wasn't much of a porch to speak of, so I unlocked the door and went straight inside.

Sam barely shut the door behind her before she hounded me with round two of the interrogation. "What did you and Griff talk about?"

"Nothing," I said. She crossed her arms and I shrugged.

"Nothing? Why would you call and then talk about nothing? Did you ask him about the woman he took to lunch?"

"No. By the way, do you know anyone named Kendra?" I asked.

"I think we have a distant cousin named Kendra," Sam chewed on her lip. "They moved somewhere up north when we were kids."

A cousin! My jubilant heart latched onto the thought. *Long-lost cousins going to lunch. That's fine.*

"Oh! I also remember a Kendra Martindale. She started out in our school, but eventually, her parents enrolled her in a prep school and fast-tracked a law degree."

And just like that, my heart deflated. *I can't compete with a swanky, sophisticated, gorgeous lawyer.*

"Why do you ask?" Sam wanted to know.

I gave in and divulged the short phone call. "Griff was joined by your mother and someone named Kendra," I finished. "Kendra of the perky voice sounded very happy to see him," I added with more snark than may have been required. I couldn't help it. Evidently, jealousy wasn't a pretty color on me.

"Don't worry. Even if my brother did share a meal with Kendra, and Kendra is the same woman he previously took to lunch when he was supposed to be out of town on business, and even if Kendra and my mother are acquainted, I'm sure it isn't as bad as it sounds," Sam did her best to sound reassuring, but somehow managed to have the opposite effect.

"Let's just go make some dessert," I told her. "You're right about one thing: worrying is doing me no good right now."

We arrived back at the dining cabin by ten. The lunch caterers hadn't arrived yet, but we did interrupt the cleaning crew. When I say interrupt, wow, did we ever! Sam and I walked in to the sound of yelling and banging noises. Rushing to the kitchen, I was nearly knocked over by a young woman as she stormed out of the kitchen, rolling her eyes at the yelling that followed her. The soft blue cleaning uniform and frumpy tan apron did nothing to hide the beauty of the black-haired woman who bumped hard into my shoulder and never looked up. Not even a muttered apology – she kept going right out the cabin door and turned down the path toward the main office and the road.

Sam and I stood in a slight shock and I couldn't help but notice the building had gone quite silent, a stark contrast to the clamor when we arrived.

"I'm sorry," an older woman with short, graying hair peeled herself away from the group in the kitchen. "We didn't know you would be back so soon. Five minutes and I promise we will be out of the way," she said with a smile.

That must be Roy's wife, I thought. *Had she been the one yelling or was it another of the younger women? What was that all about anyway?* The cleaning crew had things sparkling and were out the door in less than the promised five minutes.

"That was weird," I said as I pulled several containers of fruit from the fridge. "Did you see that woman nearly knock me down?"

"Yeah, she must have been really upset to stomp out of here like that. I think she got fired."

"Really? Why do you say that?" I asked.

"Well," Sam said, "I could be wrong but I thought I saw the gray-haired lady yelling at the other girl not to come back."

"Yikes." I shook my head. Curious as I might be, I knew it really wasn't our business. Our business was to get the desserts going. "Who knows? I do know a lot of people who are going to want snacks and desserts later. Do you want to start your Pecan Pie Cookies while I work on baking our pie crusts and mixing up some fillings?"

"Sounds good," Sam nodded. She fashioned herself an area for mixing on one end of the counter near the pantry full of dry ingredients. "After I finish these, how about I start on the Coconut Cream Hand Pies?"

"Perfect!" We worked in comfortable silence for an hour, the only words exchanged requests to pass certain ingredients. We weren't going to overdo it, only five desserts for after lunch. I allowed my mind to wander as I sifted and stirred. I felt foolish for my reaction to Griff having lunch with someone – had I not agreed to have lunch with Landon soon myself? And what exactly was going on with Landon? He seemed flaky, here a moment and gone the next, popping up unexpectedly, not to mention the strange visit to a massage parlor after hours and the mysterious tube of lipstick he dropped. I didn't know what it all meant, but I worried about my old friend.

A tapping sounded on the door frame and I looked up, surprised to find the gray-haired woman smiling at us from the dining area. I hadn't even heard her enter. "Hello," I said.

"Hi," she said as she walked on into the kitchen. "I wanted to apologize again for earlier and introduce myself. My name is Alice, I'm Roy's wife and the caretaker for The Cove's Cabins."

I shook the hand she offered as did Sam after wiping hers clean on a tea towel. "I'm Piper, this is Sam."

"It's nice to meet you, Alice," Sam added. "Thank you for taking care of the cleaning and the dishes. That makes it much faster for us to prepare all of the desserts for this afternoon."

"We hope everything is okay this morning?" I asked, hoping she would shed some light on the yelling match we had interrupted. Unfortunately for me, Alice didn't appear to be a gossip.

"Yes, thank you, everything will be fine," she said smoothly. I noticed she said *will* rather than *is* but I decided not to push the issue.

"Would you like a cookie?" Sam asked, gesturing to the rack of cooling Pecan Pie Cookies.

Smart, I thought, *people always chat over cookies.*

"Thank you but no, I have diabetes," Alice said shortly, dashing my hopes again. "I also came to inquire as to what time we should come to clean after lunch and when you will need back into the kitchen before the evening meal?" She spoke kindly, but with a professional air that did not invite new friendships.

"Good question," Sam said.

"We bake, we eat, we refill the desserts...." I used my fingers to tic things off as I thought about the day before us. "I think we could safely say we won't need to be in the kitchen between two and four this afternoon."

"Two it is," Alice nodded. "Have a good day." Without waiting for a response, she left through the dining area and out the front door.

"Okay then," I mumbled.

"You know what that means?" Sam grinned. "Two free hours for us this afternoon. Whatever are we going to do?"

"I'm sure we will think of something," I winked. Sam and I never had a problem finding ways to while away the time. We had a whole beach outside, plus the Griff and Landon conundrums to solve. *Not to mention checking in on the girls and the Ooey Gooey Bakery*, the thought sprung to mind. "Let's be sure to call Gladys and check in again," I said to Sam so that I wouldn't forget.

"Good idea. Maybe things are going smoother now."

A scratching sound at the back door startled us and Sam cracked the door open. "Hi Roy," she opened the door further. "Come on in."

"Afternoon ladies," Roy said, tipping an imaginary hat our way. "I was puttering through on my golf cart and couldn't help but smell something scrumdiddlyumptious in here."

"Help yourself," I told him. "We have lots of pies and pastries to choose from already: Peanut Butter Pie, Strawberry Cream Macarons, Watermelon Pie, and Pecan Pie Cookies."

"The Coconut Cream Hand Pies are in the oven," Sam said.

"Watermelon pie, you say? How in the world do you make a watermelon into a pie?" Roy scratched his head.

"Try a slice," Sam offered, placing a small sliver of the cold dessert on a paper plate. I handed him a fork.

Roy licked his lips after a couple of forkfuls of pie. "I'll be darned – I guess you can make watermelon into pie," he chuckled. "How do you make it so rich and creamy around all of the watermelon chunks?"

"Are you asking for our secret recipe?" Sam teased.

I laughed along with them both. "It's simple really," I explained. "Boil watermelon gelatin and mix with frozen whipped topping."

"That doesn't sound hard at all," Roy shook his head.

"No. And Roy," I added as an afterthought. "I bet Alice could find all of the things to make it sugar-free."

"You met my Alice then?" he asked.

"Yes," Sam smiled. "And she told us she was diabetic. Piper's right though, I bet Alice could whip up a sugar-free watermelon pie if she gets a sweet tooth."

"Maybe so, maybe so," Roy seemed to be thinking it over. "I'd best be getting back to work now. I'll send Alice by for the recipe if she wants it."

We waved to Roy out the back door then returned to our stations. Sam bent to get the hand pies out of the oven while I removed cookies from the cooling rack to a large platter.

"What can I do to help?" I asked Sam after all of the cookies were plated. "We have plenty of time before I need to slice the pies to be put on individual plates."

"If you could melt the chocolate to drizzle over the Coconut Cream Hand Pies, that would be great! I used up the chocolate I melted earlier on the Pecan Pie Cookies."

"No problem." I poured a bag full of chocolate chips into a glass bowl and popped it into the microwave for forty seconds. A bang came from the front door. *Who in the world could that be?* I wondered. Looking at the clock I saw it wasn't quite time for the caterers to arrive yet; we had been told they would come in at a quarter to twelve and it was only half past eleven right now.

The woman from earlier, the one with the coal-black hair who had left upset, tiptoed into the kitchen. She had a backpack purse slung over one shoulder and the most delicate Asian features. No wonder the uniform hadn't hid her beauty. Petite and exotic, she was stunning. Her eyes widened at the sight of Sam and me and she came to an abrupt stop. "Oh!" she exclaimed. "I think I left my phone earlier. Can I look around?" She didn't wait for an answer but moved with speed to the pantry and poked around, scooting ingredients back and forth.

"We haven't seen any phone," I said, frowning. This woman was either very rude or simply had the worst people skills I'd ever seen.

"Okay then. Must be somewhere else," she said. Tucking a long strand of dark hair behind her ear, she shrugged and left.

I frowned. "Who looks for their phone in the pantry?" I wondered aloud.

"What?" Sam asked.

"Nothing, I just thought that was strange. Maybe getting caught talking on the phone is why her boss yelled at that girl earlier," I mused.

"Maybe so," Sam said.

BANG!

"What was that?"

"I don't know," I said. "It sounded like it was out back."

I opened the door and was shocked to find the woman who had literally just left through the front standing outside.

"Sorry," she said. "I, uh, came back because those cookies smelt so good. Think I could snag one?" She shrugged her shoulders and one side of her lip quirked into an embarrassed smile.

"Sure, I guess so," I said slowly.

Sam appeared behind me with two cookies on a napkin. "Here you go," she offered.

"Thanks!" the girl grabbed them and literally took off running.

"Is there a sign on the door that says 'Please, the kitchen is open to anyone who is bored'?" Sam asked.

"I'm thinking we should have locked the door," I rolled my eyes.

Sam stood in the pantry, scooting ingredients around on the shelves. "Hey," she called after a moment. "Where did that open bag of powdered sugar go? I thought we still had over half of one."

I looked around the countertops. "Not out here," I told her. "I guess we used it faster than we thought?" It came out as a question. *Odd*, I thought. *We usually keep track of how fast we use things so we can stock back up.*

"I guess so. It'll be fine, I think the last bag should get us through tomorrow."

"Let's hope so," I agreed.

After another minute or two of heating the chocolate, only thirty seconds at a time, it was finally melted enough to pour. I drizzled hand pies while Sam sprinkled additional coconut flakes over the top to stick in the chocolate.

"Perfect!" she beamed when we finished.

"And just in time," I added. "Look who's here." We watched as a team of six carried in tables, tablecloths, and assorted metal stands. The catering company had arrived.

Chapter 14

"I'm starving!" I said for the third time since the caterers had set up all of the food.

Sam laughed. "You've eaten at least five cookies in the past hour. You can't possibly be starving."

"Come on," I argued, "you can't tell me all of those rich smells aren't making you ready to quit and take a lunch break." I put my hands on my hips and waited for Sam to deny it.

"Fine. Maybe I'm getting hungry, too."

"Ha! I knew it." I stuck my tongue out at Sam and grinned. "Now, let's go get a plate and eat."

The line of Breaking Chains employees had dwindled down to almost non-existent. Sam and I stepped behind the last two.

"What are you going to have?" Sam asked, eyeing the buffet arrangement of silver warming dishes that overflowed from the two rectangular tables. It was a self-serve setup; the caterers were to return later to do tear-down, clean-up, and collect the equipment.

I shook my head looking over the choices. Fried chicken, fried shrimp, green beans in a silky cheese sauce, skin-on garlic roasted red potatoes and bell peppers, salad greens, fluffy brown rolls, a Cajun rice, and creamy white gravy all vied for my attention.

"Earth to Piper," Sam nudged me with her elbow. "I thought you were starving, so, what are you going to eat?"

"Everything!"

~

I pushed my empty plate away and groaned. "I'm so full! I'm never eating again."

Sam hung her head and shook it back and forth with an exasperated sigh. "You didn't have to actually have one of everything."

"It all looked so good," I said, crossing my arms and jutting my lip out in a pout.

"Knock-knock," said a man, accompanied by tapping on the frame of the wide opening. Dressed in a dark business suit and geometric tie, he didn't fit in with the rest of the group who were wearing casual jeans and shorts with short-sleeved shirts for the afternoon.

"I'm sorry, did you need something?" I asked him.

"I wondered, do you have any more of that Peanut Butter Pie?" he asked.

I didn't even have to glance around the kitchen to know that answer. The Peanut Butter Pie had been our biggest hit. "No, unfortunately we don't. Every last slice has been picked up."

"Maybe you can find someone willing to trade," Sam said. "We have a few Coconut Cream Hand Pies left still." She handed him two plates through the opening in the wall.

"Maybe so," he murmured a quick thanks and returned to the tables.

The front door of the cabin burst open and a strong breeze blew through the dining area.

"Storm's coming!" Roy stood in the doorway, hollering. After several attempts, most of the dining room quieted and turned to pay attention. As the din of conversation and the clanking of silverware died down, a furious howling could be heard outside. Noise like sandpaper caught my ear as the wind tossed sand along the sides of the building in tiny spirals.

"A storm?" Sam asked. "I had no idea it was even supposed to rain today."

The metallic ping of large raindrops pelting the metal roof began just as conversation took off again. The noise level grew outrageous as the rain strengthened and diners scurried from chairs toward the door. Where they planned to go, or why, didn't concern me. Personally, I planned to stay nice and dry right here. Going to my cabin could wait until the storm moved on. That was the thing about the coast, storms popped up and blew in frequently. Some lasted longer than others, but most that blew through in the afternoon were small and short-lived.

"Sam, maybe we should bake more of the cookie dough from the fridge. If people are going to be stuck in here waiting out the rain, they may want more snacks." I got up and headed to the fridge as I spoke.

"Good idea," she nodded, also standing up.

The lights overhead flickered once, twice, three times before the kitchen and adjoining dining area were plunged into blackness. Unable to see a thing, I banged my hip on the corner of the worktable and let out a sharp cry of pain. Startled voices and a shriek or two sounded from the diners. Thin beams of sunlight flickered in and out of the windows between the rolling clouds. Dark outlines of people scuffling about, could be seen.

"Are you okay?" Sam asked me.

"I'll be fine. May have a small bruise, otherwise no big deal." I groped my way along the tabletop until I felt Sam's warmth next to me and stopped.

"How long do you think the power will be out?" she asked.

"No idea. I hope not long."

The door opened, another wild breeze stirred through the cabin, and the door banged shut. There was no way to tell in the dark if it had been someone coming or going. People began digging out cell phones, not as many as you would expect because evidently part of the wellness retreat was a break from technology; still, the few rebels in the dining hall switched on their flashlight apps and soon a fair amount of light filled the room.

Enough light to see the man face down in a slice of Peanut Butter Pie, not moving.

Chapter 14

"Kyle. Kyle, c'mon man!" a voice could be heard repeating in a panic.

Two or three others at the table noticed the eerie stillness of their dinner companion. Someone leaned in and felt for a pulse.

"He's dead."

Shocked whispers rippled through the crowd. A few screams shrieked above the thunder.

"Dead?" Sam asked me in a shaky voice. "Did someone say dead?"

"Yeah. It's hard to see from in here, especially without the electricity on, but I think that's the business suit guy who asked if we had any more Peanut Butter Pie." I gulped. It was sad to think that only moments ago I may have spoken to the deceased man.

"I wonder if he had a heart attack or something?" Sam asked.

It took around fifteen minutes for emergency vehicles to arrive and by then the rain had stopped, the winds were calming down. Someone had thankfully dialed 911 and by the time they arrived the crowd had backed away, leaving ample space between them and the body.

"Why are the lights off?" barked a round police officer as he bumped into a chair.

"The storm knocked out the power," a woman answered. I recognized her from the volleyball game, her name was Naomi.

"The power is on all over the city. In fact, the power is on all over this place; every cabin we drove past had lights on except this one." The officer crossed his arms as people flocked to the windows to see the surrounding cabins.

Roy shined his light on the wall and flipped the switch. On. Off. On. Off. Nothing happened. "Nope," he said. "We've got no power. Let me go check the breaker box." Roy shuffled through the dining room, skirting chairs and tables one slow step at a time, and finally made his way through the kitchen.

I followed him to the back door. "Do you need any help?" I asked.

In the dimness I saw Roy nod. "You can hold this light," he said, handing me his phone. Outside, Roy walked several feet down the side of the cabin to a large silver box was mounted to the exterior wall.

I held the phone's flashlight pointed at the box, trying not to shine it in Roy's eyes at the same time. Glancing around I saw patches of light streaming from cabin windows down the path. Roy's grumbling caught my ear and my attention returned in time to see him flipping breaker after breaker, including the large main breaker at the top.

Turning my head, I saw the interior of the kitchen and dining area remained dark except for the many phones bobbing around like oversized fireflies.

Roy rejoined me in the kitchen, shaking mud off of his feet. "Don't know why it won't work," he said as I handed his phone back to him.

"Me neither Roy, but we better go tell everyone."

Sam, Roy, and I stepped into the dining area with the others. With the clouds moving on and the large windows, the room was well-lit with natural light now. Several men and women were stacking chairs to the side while another group moved tables. They all worked to clear a path for the stretcher being rolled inside to collect the body.

Sam hurried to find and bring the police officer over to speak with us. I used the few minutes of waiting to observe the room. Soft sounds of the door opening and shutting accompanied those who were trickling out to return to their own cabins or wandering to see if the storm washed up any treasures onto the beach. A handful of others remained, eyes glued to the body at the table.

Landon had been standing near the body of business-suit-guy and walked over to where Roy and I stood to get out of the way of the coroner.

"Hey," I put a hand on his arm. "How are you holding up? Did you know him?"

Landon drew in a long, deep breath. "I did. In fact, he trained me. He was my boss."

"Your boss?" I shook my head in the hopes that if I rattled this information around it would make sense somehow.

Before Landon could respond, the police officer walked up with Sam right in step behind him.

"Show me the breaker box," the officer barked. Talk about grumpy, I guess this guy really didn't like getting out in the rain or something.

Our little entourage, Sam, Landon, Roy, myself, and Officer Grumpy, trekked back through the dark kitchen. I opened the door to do the honors. The rest of us leaned out the door and watched.

"Your boss?" I whispered to Landon.

"Yes, my boss. I work for Breaking Chains but it isn't something I advertise."

"What?" Sam asked trying to hear. "You're going into advertising?"

"Get inside!" Officer Grumpy suddenly shouted. "Don't make more footprints." He got on his radio next. "Rawlins, secure the building. The power has been cut." Crackling and a voice came back but the words were drowned out as Roy stumbled through the doorway, out of range of Officer Grumpy's mood.

Unfortunately for Roy, and us, the officer came right back inside. "Get back to the other room," he ushered us.

We high-tailed it into the dining area and stood to the side where he indicated. "Officer," I squinted and was able to pick out the name on his shirt badge, "Officer Campbell, did you say the power was cut? As in, the electricity being out was on purpose?"

"Yes," he said gruffly before going to the center of the room. An ear-piercing whistle sounded. After Officer Campbell had everyone's attention, he stared hard at each face, saying at last, "Nobody is to leave until after statements are taken. If someone who sat at your table is not here, you need to give their name to my deputy so we can find and speak to them as well. This death will be investigated as a potential crime."

A crescendo of whispers broke out.

"You can't keep us here," an outraged voice erupted from the crowd.

"I thought he had a heart attack," a woman a few feet from my left whispered. I lifted my hands in a gesture of *who knows* and shook my head.

"Form a line," Officer Campbell said. "My deputy will take your statement on the porch as you exit. One at a time," he emphasized.

Chapter 15

I rubbed the raised chill bumps on my arms. It was June. On the beach. On the beach in the south to be specific. It wasn't even close to cold outside, but still, I shivered. I couldn't stop thinking of that poor man. Dead. Murdered? I didn't know for sure, yet the police intended to investigate all possibilities.

I had given my statement to the deputy on the porch, followed in close succession by Sam and Landon. The questions had been brief and my responses even more so:

Did you know the victim? *No.*

Did you bake the desserts? *Yes.*

Did you serve the victim Peanut Butter Pie? *No, we were out.*

How did he get Peanut Butter Pie then? *I don't know.*

Did you have any reason to harm the victim? *No.*

Did you see the victim arguing with anyone? *No.*

The deputy told each of us not to leave The Cove's Cabins in case the police had any more questions. Landon made his way towards the rolling surf. Sam and I followed.

"Landon," I put a hand on his arm. "Are you okay?"

"Yes. No. I don't know," he shook his head.

"You said that man was your boss. What was his name?" I knew sometimes it helped to talk through things. I also felt more than a bit of curiosity at Landon's involvement with Breaking Chains. He certainly hadn't mentioned it, not that we'd had a lot of time to chat since he turned up.

"Arthur. Arthur Cole was his name."

"So, you worked for Breaking Chains?" Sam asked the obvious question for us both.

"Yeah, I'm not an office employee or anything, but my team reported to Arthur."

"I'm sorry for your loss," I told him.

"That's the thing," Landon said. "I didn't even like the guy. Don't get me wrong, he seemed like a good boss and I learned a lot from him. We weren't exactly friends though. Breaking Chains is all about helping the victims but to Arthur, it was no more than a regular business. He didn't have any real empathy or contact with the people we helped bring in off of the streets. The only reason he even sat at my table was that he wanted to trade desserts with me."

"Everybody has their strengths," Sam said with a light tone. "Maybe Arthur only felt comfortable with his skills for the business end of things?"

"I guess," Landon conceded.

A scream, high-pitched and terrified, had us each whipping our necks down the beach to the left. A few other people heard and jogged toward a woman who kept screaming and scuttled backward in the sand like a crab as fast as she could go. She tried to stand but couldn't seem to regain her footing. She kept crawling backward, her eyes never leaving something in the edge of the waves.

"You think she saw a jellyfish or a shark or something?" I asked.

That theory evaporated seconds later.

"A body!" someone near her called. "Get the police down here, there's a body."

"Sam, hurry and get the police," I told her. Our group still huddled closest to the dining cabin and she could get there fastest. She sped toward the cabin and the officers taking statements.

I took off toward the frightened woman and the body. Don't ask me why; I spent the whole minute it took to get there asking myself what in the world I thought I could do to help. I could hear Landon's steps thudding behind me and soon he overtook me with his longer stride.

When we got close, we saw someone attempting CPR on a woman. The figure sprawled too still, her ebony hair tangled with seaweed and spotted with sand. Up the shore a bit, the little round man who had led the prayer at lunch sat with the lady who spotted the body first. He talked soft and nodded, patting her arm every so often to try and comfort her. Given that the screaming stopped, I'd say he was doing a good job.

The man doing CPR rocked back on his heels, shaking his head in defeat.

I gasped at the first unimpeded sight of the woman's face. I recognized her.

The girl from the cleaning crew!

Before I could react, Landon also gasped beside me. The blood drained from his face faster than water from my tub.

"Coco," he whispered.

"What?" I asked.

"Nothing. I've gotta go," Landon took off running again, this time up through the cabins.

"Wait, we aren't supposed to leave," I tried to catch him but a pain in my side pulled me up short. *Geeze,* I thought holding my left hand to my ribs. *I've really need to start exercising, this is ridiculous.*

Officer Campbell and his deputy passed me on the way to the beach. They slowed at the sight of me gasping; I waved them on down to the body.

"Piper, are you okay?" Sam came alongside me and asked.

"I am. I'm not sure about Landon though."

"What do you mean? I don't see him."

"That's what I mean. I'm worried. He is acting strange and, well, I hate to think it but I'm wondering if he is into some kind of trouble."

"How so?" Sam asked as we linked arms and settled into a much slower walk back to our cabin. The pain in my side was easing, thank goodness.

"He knew the guy, Arthur, who died in the dining cabin," I wheeled through the worries in my mind.

"Right. He explained that," Sam nodded.

"Turns out, he knew the dead girl on the beach, too. At least, he seemed to." I explained about him saying 'Coco' before dashing off. "He became extremely upset and took off running."

"What are you saying?" Sam asked. "Do you think we need to tell Officer Campbell?"

"Not yet. I'm saying it may be time to do some digging."

Chapter 16

"This is a terrible plan," Sam grumbled, unbuckling her seat belt.

I looked around the parking lot of the massage parlor. "Hey, at least it's daylight. It'll be fine, come on."

"Why in the world did I let you talk me into this?" she grouched.

"Don't you blame me; I told you that you needed to let me do this alone."

"Fat chance I was letting that happen."

I grinned. Sam might be mad at me, but she would do whatever it took to look out for me. Even if that meant going to chat with the people at the seedy massage parlor Landon visited in the sketchy neighborhood we had vowed to avoid.

We tried to act casual as we strolled to the door. Today, the neon open sign was flashing green in the window, though the blinds were still closed.

"Do we knock or just go in?" Sam hesitated at the door.

"They say open." I grabbed the doorknob and turned. The moment the door opened I started coughing. "Apparently," I said trying to get my breath back, "they let you smoke in here."

The stench in the tiny foyer area had me breathing through my mouth. I'm not an expert, having never experimented with drugs myself, but I was pretty sure it wasn't just cigarettes polluting all of the perfectly good oxygen around us.

"Horrible idea," Sam's short whisper sounded harsh and she cut her eyes at me, crossing her arms over her chest.

I raised my shoulders in an apologetic shrug.

Sam dropped her arms and plastered a smile on her face. Knowing she wouldn't be letting go that easy, I looked behind me. A thin Asian woman with a smooth face and tight smile approached from the hallway.

"We help you?" she asked, her accent making the words come out in quick clips.

I nodded. "We came here looking for someone," I told him.

"You both want massage?" she pointed back and forth to us.

"No, no thank you," I shook my head.

"Who massage? You?" she asked, her lips pursed.

I shook my head no. "No. You don't understand…" I tried again but again he interrupted.

"You massage." She smiled at Sam as if figuring it out. "Follow me." With that she turned and led the way down a narrow hall, not looking back to see if we were coming.

I grimaced at Sam and tugged her down the hall, nearly trotting to catch up to the woman ahead of us. We passed two doors locked with padlocks as we went.

"I'm going to kill you," Sam ground out between her teeth.

"Don't say that, we have enough dead bodies."

"Fine. I'll…I'll do something to make you regret this day, just as soon as I think of it."

"But look," I tried to pacify her, "you get a nice massage. I'll even pay for it."

She simply glared.

Oh brother, I'm gonna get it.

We stopped at a door on the left of the hallway. The woman opened it and ushered us inside. "You wait," she said, then quick as lightning exited and shut the door on us.

"Awk-ward," I sing-songed at Sam, standing next to the single massage table in the room. "Want me to turn around while you undress for your massage?" I snickered.

"If you think for one minute I'm getting on that table for a massage in this health-code violating, foul-smelling, hole-in-the-wall joint, then you have lost your mind."

I laughed out loud, couldn't help it, the indignant look on her face, complete with upper lip curled in disgust, proved too much for me to hold it together. "You sound like Deidra," I cracked up then put a hand to my mouth. *Oops, now she might really kill me.*

"I do not sound like my mother," Sam argued. "She would never approve of the use of the word 'joint' in a sentence." As we stood looking at each other, me smothering a laugh and Sam trying to remain angry, a smile tugged lightly at the corners of her lips. The absurdity of the situation won out; Sam covered her mouth to stifle her own laughter.

Two soft raps on the door preceded the entry of a much younger Asian girl with hair dyed a golden-caramel color. I couldn't believe she worked here; if asked to guess, I would have pegged her as sixteen or seventeen years old.

"Hello!" she greeted us with a smile that didn't reach her eyes. "Who is here for the massage?" Her English was excellent and hardly a trace of accent could be heard.

"Neither," I said. "We'd really like to talk about a friend of ours."

The smile disappeared. "I'm sorry. No massage, I have to go," she backed up.

"We will still pay for your time," Sam assured, causing the girl to hesitate.

"Our friend, he came here late last night. We think he might be in some trouble." I met the girl's eyes as I spoke in a low, soft voice. I hoped to put her at ease; right now, she resembled a frightened rabbit, poised to bounce at the first sign of danger.

"I didn't work last night," she glanced to the door and back to us, still unsure.

"Okay, no problem," Sam said. "Could you tell us someone who did?"

"Mamasan," the girl whispered. "Mamasan is always here. And I think last night would have been Red and Coco on shift."

I darted a glance at Sam; she raised her eyebrows.

"Coco?" I asked. A bad feeling swirled in the pit of my stomach and I found myself leaning toward the girl, on the edge of my seat.

"Yes. But Coco isn't here today. I think Red might be here later. I don't know if she would talk to you."

"What's your name?" Sam asked.

"You can call me BeeBee," she refused to meet our eyes.

"BeeBee," I swallowed past the tightness in my throat. "Can you tell me what Coco looks like?"

The air-conditioner chose that moment to kick on, the loud noise as it struggled to run causing Sam and I to jump. BeeBee, I noticed, flinched and closed her eyes, making herself smaller for just a moment before she gave a slight shake and relaxed.

"Sure, yeah. Coco is beautiful, tiny, gorgeous black hair, this perfect pert little nose." BeeBee tugged at the hem of her shirt. "Listen, my boss is gonna be mad if I'm not working."

"BeeBee," Sam spoke with sadness. "Coco was found dead this morning."

"Dead?" All of the color drained from BeeBee's face. She wrapped her arms around herself in a hug, trying to insulate herself from the news. "No, she can't be dead. She can't be. I told her not to leave."

"What do you mean?" I asked.

BeeBee narrowed her eyes. Her voice came out a harsh whisper and she moved closer to us, glancing over her shoulder at the door. "You said you came to ask about your friend. Now you say Coco is dead. I don't believe it. What does this have to do with your friend? Why are you really here?"

"Like I said, our friend came here last night. We saw him enter after the open sign had been switched off," I explained. "Today, a woman's body turned up on the beach. The same woman had been in an argument with someone at The Cove's Cabins earlier in the day. Our friend Landon, when he saw the body, he got upset and said the name Coco before taking off."

"Wait," BeeBee held her hand up for me to stop. "You said your friend's name is Landon?"

"Yes," I nodded.

"Do you know him?" Sam asked, gripping the arm of her chair.

"Maybe. Kind, handsome, sandy hair?" BeeBee looked at us. At our fervent nodding she went on, "Yes, Landon came here often. He was a," she looked upward as if searching the ceiling for a word. "Special client. Yes, he was a special client," she smiled and this time her face softened.

I gasped, shocked and full of discomfort. ATMs. Open after dark to "special clients". Gorgeous girls taking shifts. The overkill locks on the doors. Everything slid into place. We were in a cleverly disguised brothel!

Sam covered her mouth with both hands.

"No!" BeeBee shook her head, waving her hands back and forth. "No, he was not a happy ending client," BeeBee clarified.

Well, I thought, *now we know the nature of service the Thai Massage does indeed provide.* I shuddered.

"What kind of client was he then?" I dug my fingernails into my palms, unsure I wanted the answer but needing to know it regardless.

"Landon brought gifts. He tried to help us, help the girls. He did not come for any massages."

Chapter 17

"Okay then." I said, sliding into the driver's seat of my truck and locking the door. We both sat in silence a few moments, absorbing the basics of what BeeBee had been able to tell us.

"That proved to be informative," Sam said at last.

"Are you admitting that I had a good idea?" I clutched at my heart, feigning shock.

"Nope." Sam shook her head. "I'm just saying that maybe it is good we found out more before mentioning our concerns about Landon to the police."

"I'm glad we were wrong about him. I feel terrible that I suspected him of being involved in illegal activities, and all because we saw him go there after closing hours then I found that tube of lipstick."

"You couldn't have known the phone number on the lipstick would be a hotline to help women who wanted to escape from the life of prostitution, dancing, or sex trafficking organizations," Sam pointed out reasonably.

"True. I'm so glad to know Breaking Chains cares about the victims and provides resources and shelter to get those out who need help and have nowhere to go."

"And I'm relieved to know it is part of Landon's job to visit the bars, sport clubs, and massage houses suspected of trafficking every month," Sam admitted. "I really enjoyed hanging out with him for volleyball and was really upset when we thought he came here as a client and maybe even hurt that poor Coco girl on the beach."

"Speaking of which, none of this explains why Landon ran off so fast when her body washed up," I cranked the truck. "I hope he turns up so we can talk to him. Right now, we have to get back in time to make desserts for after supper, assuming the retreat is still going the rest of the weekend."

"Right." Sam pulled out her phone. "I think that I'll just check in on Gladys and the girls one more time while you drive."

"Nervous?" I shot a sideways look to Sam but she held up a finger. Gladys had answered the phone.

"Hey, Gladys." Sam's smile stretched. "Piper and I were checking in. How are things?"

I turned the radio off. Drat. Still unable to hear Gladys's side of the conversation, I drove quietly and waited.

Hanging up, Sam put the phone back in her purse. "The firemen were back."

"What?!" My heart skittered in my chest. I started to pull over.

"For cookies. The firemen were back for cookies." Sam had the grace to look guilty. "Sorry, I didn't mean to freak you out."

I breathed easier again. "I'm not sure we should cater weekend events in the future. My heart might not be able to take it."

~

Parking by the main office on our return to The Cove's Cabins, I grabbed the grocery sack of powdered sugar and butter out of the back seat. Sam had remembered we were running low, and we ended up with just enough time to buy them and still get back by four.

Roy and his golf cart were nowhere to be seen so we set out on foot down the path toward the dining cabin. Here and there we passed small groups of people walking. Others sat on porches of the residential cabins, talking in low voices as we passed by.

We rounded the last curve of the path and I stopped short. Bright yellow crime scene tape hung in a crisp, straight line blocked our entrance to the dining cabin and the kitchen. Honestly, I guess I should have seen that coming; instead, it took my breath away. The body. Both bodies, terrible as they were, hadn't hit me as hard as this bright yellow beacon screaming to the world that death had been here, that evil snuck in and snuck out in the dark storm and left the rest of us to deal with the mess.

"Now what?" Sam asked.

I barely registered the sound of footsteps before someone collided into me from behind. I stumbled forward as several hands steadied me, Sam's and those of the woman who had nearly knocked me down.

"I'm terribly sorry!" The woman patted me down as if to ensure she hadn't broken me. "I was looking at the ocean when I jogged around the corner."

Taking a step back, I waved off her concern. "It's okay. We shouldn't have stopped in the middle of the path." I searched my memory for why she looked familiar. *That's right, she's the Dark Chocolate Chip pancake lady, the one with the tight bun in her hair.* I hadn't recognized her because now she looked disheveled and distracted as opposed to the poised figure she had presented at breakfast. I racked my brain for a name. *Regina!*

"No. It is my fault; I should pay more attention," Regina said.

Just then the chaplain also came upon our little group. "It's the delicious dessert ladies!" he exclaimed, shaking first Sam's hand and then mine, pumping so hard I nearly dropped the bag of groceries.

My phone rang then, interrupting, and I glanced at the screen. Gladys's name blinked on the caller ID. "I really need to take this," I apologized to Regina and the chaplain. I took a few steps away, the grocery sack now dangling from my elbow and bouncing off my hip.

"Hello," I answered the phone.

"Piper, hi dearie," Gladys chirped, cheerful as ever. "Listen, I hate to bother you but Millie has an art project due Monday and not very much time to work on it since she's working here."

"Does she need time off?" I asked.

Sam walked toward me; Regina continued her jog going off the path and further into the dunes. I must have missed the chaplain taking his leave.

"Actually, I told her you probably wouldn't mind at all if she did her homework on the tables here in the café," Gladys explained. "She insisted I call and get your permission though."

"Sure, sure. I don't mind if she does her homework," I became distracted from the conversation when I noticed Officer Grumpy, I mean Campbell, making his way toward us. His scowl seemed deeper than ever.

"Piper Rivers and Samantha Lowe?" he asked. Two deputies broke from his shadow and flanked us.

"Gladys," I said. "I think I'm going to have to let you go." I hung up the phone without waiting to see if she heard me.

"How can we help you officer?" Sam asked with a smile.

Officer Campbell's features did not warm. Instead, he narrowed his eyes. "Did you two leave The Cove's Cabins this afternoon?"

"Yes, but only to check on some things about our friend Landon," Sam nodded.

Inwardly I groaned. It had been made very clear everyone should stay put. Why did I let my curiosity impact my decision?

"Landon Oliver?" one deputy asked, receiving a glare from Officer Campbell.

"Yes," I answered. *How did they know Landon's name?* I wondered. *Did he come back?*

"What's in the bag?" Officer Campbell pointed.

I looked down at the now-forgotten grocery bag. "This? Just a few ingredients for baking that we stopped to pick up."

"Mind if my deputy has a look?"

"Not at all," I shrugged. *Maybe once they've finished harassing Sam and me the lovely officers can move on to catching a killer*, I thought punitively.

Taking the bag from me, the deputy knelt and shook it empty on the ground.

"Hey!" I moved toward him. "My butter is going to have dirt in it."

"Sir," the deputy ignored me. "Look at this," he said. He slid his hands into gloves and then held up a small black cylinder, almost like an old-fashioned film canister, and opened the lid.

Officer Campbell sniffed and raised his eyebrows. The deputy nodded.

I looked at Sam; she shrugged, as much in the dark about what was going on as me.

Officer Campbell caught me unaware while I puzzled over the deputy and the canister. Wrenching my arms behind my back he said, "Piper Rivers, you are under the arrest for the murder of Arthur Cole."

Chapter 18

"Arrest?" I shrieked. The cuffs cinched tightly against my wrists.

"What in the world for?" Sam threw her arms up. "Piper didn't murder anyone, that's absurd."

"Get out of the way, lady," Officer Campbell growled at Sam. "If you don't pipe down, I'll arrest you for obstruction of justice in regards to a murder investigation."

"You have yet to see obstruction," Sam pulled herself up ramrod straight. "But I guarantee you're about to." Her normal pleasant smile disappeared, replaced by more of a wicked grin that promised no good things. Shoot, her look had me worried and she was on my side.

"Do you want me to stop her?" the deputy on my left asked the sheriff. Sam stomped toward the Main Office and the road, phone to her ear before she disappeared from sight.

"Nah. What's Miss Priss gonna do, she has to stay put like everyone else."

I shook my head. He had no idea how determined Sam could be.

~

The ride to my new accommodations at the Pierson County Sheriff's Department hadn't taken long. Jostling around, hands bound behind me and rubbing all manner of stickiness on the seat, bracing myself to bang against the window at any moment, the ride had been unpleasant to say the least. Beyond that, I became frustrated when all attempts to reason with or ask questions of the officer or his deputy were met with stony silence. When at last we arrived, I felt relief to be freed from the tight space of the car. The feeling didn't last.

I had no idea how long I'd been in this disgusting pit of a room but it certainly felt like an eternity. I scrunched my nose in distaste. The stench. The overwhelming smell of stale vomit, ammonia, and cleaning products that didn't quite get the job done. I'm pretty sure my nostrils might be singed and I wished desperately for the smell of fresh cookies instead. Like Dorothy in Oz, I closed my eyes and thought to myself *I'll be out soon, I'll be out soon, I'll be out soon.* With no ruby slippers to click, I found myself on the same concrete bench jutting out from the wall.

The woman next to me, busty and leaving nothing to the imagination, sneezed without covering her nose or mouth. I inched further away.

I supposed the fact that I'm still sitting in a holding cell is good. I haven't been booked, yet, so there is still time for the police to realize they've made a mistake and let me go. *God, please get me out of here, please! Lord, you know I didn't kill anyone. Please let this all be a bad dream.*

A pixie-haired woman old enough to be my grandmother padded to the holding cell and crooked a finger at me. "Rivers," she drawled.

Or not. My heart plummeted. *This is it. They're locking me up, throwing away the key. I'll never sleep in my bed again. Never eat another fresh, masterfully creative cookie again.* I flinched at the painful thought. Maybe I could beg my way into the jail kitchen as a line cook. *No, there has to be a way out.*

"Ma'am," I said to the older woman as I side-stepped a pretty angry looking teen and skirted around the woman passed out in the floor, stringy purple hair fanned out around her, drool mingling with Lord knows what other fluids on this floor as they seeped downhill toward the drain in the center of the room.

"Ma'am, I think there has been a mistake," I said as I stepped out of the cell into a narrow corridor.

"So, you don't want to go home with the hotshot out front that pulled strings to pick you up, that's fine by me sister. Step right back inside, doesn't bother me." She waved an arm at the depressing room.

"Let out?" I asked. I stepped away from the door, putting as much distance between that horrifying room and myself as possible. "No, no mistake. I'm sorry, let's go, I'll follow you." I didn't care who the hotshot was, didn't give it a second thought in fact. They were sending me home and nothing else registered in my brain like that one neon flashing piece of information.

"Shut your trap and come on; I don't have all day."

I resisted the urge to pantomime zipping my lips. Really, I'm in enough trouble, no need to push it.

"Roll doors," the old woman yelled at a camera at the end of the hall. The metal doors in front of us clanked open about an inch at a time.

I all but walked on top of the little woman when I saw the brighter light of the reception area where intakes and releases were processed. I followed my escort to a glass window fitted with a small hole above a tray just big enough to squeeze a small purse or billfold through. I signed my name on the form when asked and accepted my telephone and wallet from the gentleman on the other side.

I was then shuffled into a short line of men and women heading for a glass door beyond which I could see daylight. It appeared to be very late afternoon; the sun sat low on the horizon. *Almost free, almost out*, I repeated to myself.

"Piper!" I heard my name called out the moment my feet hit the concrete steps leading to the parking lot from the building.

I whipped my head around. There. To the right, Griff bounded toward me two steps at a time.

When he reached me, I simply crumpled into his arms. I didn't know whether I cried from relief that he came to get me or shame that anyone had to pick me up from jail period; either way, tears squeezed through my eyelashes and trickled to my chin before jumping off.

"Piper, let's get you out of here," with a gentle tug at my wrist, Griff led me out to his truck and tucked me safely into the comfy seat.

I leaned my head back with a sigh, gathering myself. Rubbing my arms, I mentally clicked delete on the images cycling through my head; images of unkempt women, unyielding faces of guards and officers, and unidentifiable substances.

"What do you want first – a shower or a milkshake?" Griff grinned at me from the driver's seat.

I laughed out loud. "Yes." Warmth spread through my whole body and my heart caught in my throat. Griff knew me better than I knew myself, he anticipated my wants and my need to be distracted from my ordeal. *Slow down*, I tried to tell my heart. The soft flutter it gave at Griff's answering laugh signaled there was little chance of my heart obeying.

Griff drove me to one of my favorite places, Marble Slab Creamery, for a massive milkshake mixed with toppings of sprinkles and Oreos. He ordered while I washed my hands and arms in the hottest water that I could coax out of the bathroom sink.

"So," I asked as we headed back to The Cove's Cabins, "how did you get me out of jail? They never even booked me, but I thought they had to do that before bail could even be posted."

"Don't know," he said. "You'll have to ask Sam. She called and told me I had to be there to pick you up and at what time; she didn't explain a thing. Would you like to paint the picture for me?"

About an hour later, I stood under scalding water in the little cabin Sam and I shared at The Cove's Cabins.

I had explained everything to Griff on the ride back. He had listened without interruption, the only sign of his agitation the tightening of his grip on the steering wheel and the white line forming around his lips as they pulled into a grim line. When I got to the part about Landon running off, he had muttered something too low for me to hear.

Sam wasn't at our cabin when we arrived. My cell was dead and Griff had forgotten his in the rush to pick me up. He offered to find her while I got cleaned up. Personally, I felt like I could shower for two days and still not be clean.

I heard voices and assumed Griff had returned with Sam. I scrubbed myself once more with the loofah. Between the heat and the number of washings, my skin glowed a bright red. Time to get out.

After I dried with a towel, I braided my hair into tiny French braids and tossed on yoga pants and a t-shirt. I didn't make it two feet out of the bathroom before Sam launched herself at me. I hugged her back, squeezing tight. "I don't know what you did, but thank you."

"It was nothing," Sam said as she stepped back.

"I beg to differ." I looked around. Griff was seated on the edge of one bunk, hunched forward to avoid hitting his head. The bed looked tiny behind his large frame. Quite an amusing sight if I had time to be amused. "Sam, seriously. How did you get me out? I thought for sure that Officer Grumpy would be arresting you for interference next."

"I'm curious as well, oh sister of mine," Griff raised an eyebrow. "Did you call Dad?"

I settled cross-legged on the floor; the bunk reminded me too much of the concrete bench sticking out from the wall and I couldn't bring myself to perch on it. Sam sat down next to me.

"Did your dad get me out of jail?" I asked, flabbergasted. Sam's parents didn't exactly like me so the thought of help from that area shocked me to the core. Guilt began to seep in, too. *Would I owe them? Oh well, it would be worth it.*

"No, Dad was in a meeting and wouldn't take my call." Sam rolled her eyes but I saw the sting of hurt cross her face.

"Maybe he had government business," I offered.

"It was his weekly golf meeting with buddies," she spat. "Don't worry about how I got you out."

"Well, now I'm gonna worry," I insisted. "Did you bribe someone? That's not like you. Did you use your dad to threaten them anyway?" I sat up straighter. "Did Officer Grumpy find the actual killer?" I asked with hope.

"No."

"Sam." Griff gave her the *big brother* look I'd seen him use on her for years. She almost always caved.

"Fine. I called Mother."

I gasped. Griff jerked back and hit his head on the bunk. Rubbing it he asked. "You called our mother? She hates Piper. Why would she help?" He looked at me, "Sorry."

"I agree, Sam, why would your mom help me? What could she even do?"

"Honestly, I don't know who she called or what took place. I don't think I want to know the details, but Mother always has influence in high places. It's her favorite thing about being the wife of the mayor."

"Back to the why…," I prompted.

"I agreed to a favor," Sam shrugged.

A favor. Oh my gosh! Deidra's going to make Sam quit the bakery. Queasiness bubbled in my stomach.

"Calm down," Sam responded to the panic evident on my face. "It isn't anything horrible. I mean, it isn't pleasant but I'll survive."

"Sam, tell us what in the world you had to promise Mother," Griff demanded.

"Sheesh." She rolled her shoulders and exhaled. "I have to go with them to next month's big shindig for all of Dad's supporters. It will be at the country club, as usual."

"Thank goodness!" They both looked at me. "I just mean, that sounds nice and boring and quick. I thought she would have insisted you quit working at the bakery."

"I also have to go with a date."

"Well, still," I drew the word out, my tone hopeful.

Shaking her head, Sam snuffed out my ounce of positivity. "It gets worse."

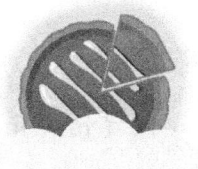

Chapter 19

"How does it get worse?" I asked.

"It has to be a date of her choosing," Sam clarified.

"Crap," I said. "Your mom gets to set you up on a blind date? That really sucks."

"I'm surprised you didn't leave Piper in jail if those were the terms," Griff joked.

I snatched a pillow off the bed behind me and chucked it at his face.

Before Griff could retaliate, loud knocking reverberated through the cabin. He held a hand out for us to stay where we were and answered the door.

"Is Piper here? Or Sam?" Landon peered around Griff.

"Come in," Sam said.

"Boy, do we need to talk to you." I nodded at Griff to open the door.

Landon glanced over his shoulder before following Griff inside the already cramped space. He locked the door behind him. "I need your help."

"Not yet you don't," Griff remained standing, arms crossed. "You owe everyone some explanations. Piper told me you ran off when the body of the woman was discovered. Why?"

"I knew her. I worried about the other girls she worked with and I was afraid someone would connect me to her so I left to try and figure some things out."

"Why did you come back?" I asked him. My neck pinched from craning my head to look up at the guys; I stood and Sam followed.

"I heard the police arrested a suspect. I figured it was safe now," Landon explained.

"I wouldn't be so sure," Sam said. "The police were curious how Piper knew you when they arrested her. They seemed interested in you."

Landon balked. "Arrested? What are you talking about? Piper, you were arrested?"

"Yeah, but Sam got me out, so it's okay now."

Sam grimaced. "Actually, Piper, I don't know how to tell you this. You aren't actually cleared yet. When they released you to Griff, they literally released you to his custody. That was the agreement Mother was able to get."

"Why? I don't understand. I didn't do anything wrong."

Griff cocked his head at Sam and frowned. "Sounds like you left out some details."

"They found evidence," Sam turned to me. "Whatever was in that little canister, the one the deputy picked up when he dumped out the grocery bag before they arrested you? They say it is poison; the same poison that laced the Peanut Butter Pie and killed Arthur Cole."

"Wait. The pie was the murder weapon?" Landon's eyes widened.

"Yes," Sam nodded.

"That's horrible," I rubbed my temples. "I can't believe my dessert was used to kill someone."

"It's worse than that," Landon said.

"How?" Griff asked.

"That pie was meant for me; someone tried to kill *me*. The only reason Arthur ate it is because we...."

"Swapped!" I finished. "That's right. I forgot Arthur wanted Peanut Butter Pie and I told him he would have to trade with someone because there were no more slices."

"Who would want to kill you?" Sam asked Landon.

234

Chapter 20

Landon shook his head. One hand on his hip, he ran the other through his sandy hair and pulled in frustration. "I don't know, at least I don't know their name. I think I know why though."

"Does this have something to do with Coco?" I asked. "With trying to help those women?"

"How did you know about that?" Landon glanced between me and Sam.

"We paid BeeBee a visit," Sam said. "Actually, first we saw you at the massage parlor…" Sam and I took turns explaining how we had gone down the rabbit hole of suspecting Landon ourselves and eventually investigating at the massage parlor.

Griff looked like he might blow a gasket any minute by the time we finished. "Are you kidding me?" His hands balled into fists at his side and a vein bulged in the crook of his elbow.

I winced. "I may have left a teensy bit out on the drive home."

"You two," he pointed, "have no business poking around places like that. Or investigating murders; good grief! What were you thinking?"

"He's right," Landon chimed in. "You put yourselves in danger. The people who run Thai Massage are bad people. I think the reason someone killed Coco and wants me dead is because someone in Breaking Chains actually runs the business. At least, that's what I think. That's what I went to talk to Coco about last night."

Sam walked the two and a half steps it took to get to the back wall and cracked the lone window open. "What?" she raised her arms up. "This cabin is stuffy, the talk of murder and murderers is making me claustrophobic, and we can't exactly go anywhere else right now."

I leaned over and tugged a cooler from the end of the bed. I passed out water bottles then Sam and I sat down on the lid. Landon took the cue and sat on the bunk opposite us. Griff leaned against the bed frame, still looking none too happy.

"Go on," I told Landon. "Tell us why you think someone you work with is running these businesses; businesses that your organization actively tries to shut down."

As we each listened to Landon's story, interjecting questions here and there, the shuffling sound at the back window went unnoticed. The shadow that passed over the panes just one more in the long shadows thrown by palms as the sun descended.

Griff used Sam's phone to call the main office and rent one of the few remaining cabins for the night before it got too late. Landon, we all decided, would bunk in there with him and try to stay out of sight.

~

By the time we woke, the dining cabin had been cleared for use. The crime scene tape, thank goodness, had been removed and was no nowhere in sight when Sam and I entered in the wee hours. Evidently the popular saying *the show must go on* also applied to corporate wellness retreats.

"Where should we start?" Sam asked.

With both hands fisted at my hips I looked around the kitchen. "Pantry," I decided. "Let's dump everything from the pantry first."

Sam and I had agreed last night that whatever ingredients remained from the police search we would throw out. Between the poison and the number of people combing ingredients on a hunt for the poison, we refused to take any risks. Everything must go. Griff had already driven into town with a long list to pick up supplies for us.

"No pancakes for breakfast if Griff doesn't make it back in time," Sam said.

"The eggs in the fridge should be safe. And we have another package of sausage that didn't get used in scones."

"We could do sausage egg muffins and some omelets."

"I think that will be perfect," I agreed as I dropped a can of baking soda into the garbage bag we were dragging through the pantry. "It's a shame what a waste all of this is. Obviously, the poison had to be put on just that one slice of pie because nobody else got sick."

"Yeah," Sam nodded. "Most of these ingredients are probably perfectly safe." Sam glanced past my shoulder to the pantry door then said, dropping her voice to a whisper, "How are we going to help Landon clear his name?"

"You mean since he and Griff told us specifically to stay out of it?" I whispered back. Both men had been adamant that they didn't want either of us in danger. "And why are we whispering?"

"I just don't want anyone to overhear us."

"I locked the door," I told her without whispering. "If anyone is going to come in, they have to have a key and we would hear them first."

Sam chuckled. "I guess we don't have to whisper then. Anyway, we have to do something right? I mean, Landon can't exactly be out in the open when both the police and a murderer are after him."

"True." We went back to working, lost in thought for a bit. "I know, let's make a list of the people who most likely had access to poison the pie."

"Okay," Sam dusted her hands on her apron and took the garbage bag from me. "Go get your notebook; I know it's here somewhere," she laughed, always finding my list-making obsession both humorous and handy. Tying up the ends of the garbage bag, she hauled it to the back door to be collected later.

We sat down at the work island. "Let's start with all of the people who were in the kitchen," I said.

"Coco, though it would be strange if she tried to kill Landon when he only tried to help her," Sam pointed out.

"Unless she didn't want out," I said, writing Coco at the top of the *Pie Poisoner* list. "And really, that means we need to put the whole cleaning crew on the list. They were all in the kitchen while we were gone, including Roy's wife Alice."

"I'll see if I can get the names of the other girls from Alice or Roy," Sam volunteered. "Speaking of, should we put Roy on the list?"

"He does have a key."

"And he was poking around out back before he came in for dessert. Maybe we stopped him before he cut the power on his first try."

"We still don't have a motive for half of these people."

"Is that it though, for the list I mean?"

"Nope," I shook my head. "I think we need to add the people at Landon's table. They would have been closest to the slice of pie itself after it reached Landon."

"I hate to be Devil's advocate," Sam said, "but we probably need to keep Landon's name on the list for now. He said he didn't get along with his boss, he had access to the pie, and it seems odd that he hasn't cleared things up with Officer Campbell if he's innocent."

"Ha! Like Officer Grumpy would listen to reason. Fine," I conceded, scribbling away in my notebook. "Landon is on the list, too. I'll get the names of others seated at his table after breakfast."

"Whew, this is exhausting."

"We haven't even started the list for who might have killed Coco…"

Rattling sounded at the front door, followed by three sharp knocks. Sam and I jumped.

I put a finger to my lips. Sam nodded. Together, we tiptoed from the kitchen through the dining hall and peered out the corner of a window. I fingered the pocket knife that sat heavy in my cargo pants.

"Good grief, it's just Griff," I whooshed out a breath. *When did I get so jumpy?*

Chapter 21

Breakfast had been a somber occasion. The pancakes and sausage-egg muffins were appreciated, but conversation didn't flourish as it did yesterday. The little round man who had been consoling the woman on the beach yesterday turned out to be the chaplain for Breaking Chains. During breakfast he stood and spoke kind words over Arthur Cole, encouraging others to come and share stories as well. It turned into a beautiful memorial with a special prayer at the end asking that the police would solve the investigation soon.

"How sad," I muttered aloud as Sam and I stacked dirty dishes in the sink.

"Yeah, it is terrible. His coworkers all seemed like they really liked Arthur."

"No," I shook my head, "not that. I mean, yes, that too, but I was thinking how sad it was that nobody mentioned Coco. Besides Landon, nobody here seemed to know her. Who knows if she has family, or if they've been notified? I can't get the picture of her out of my mind; tossed up from the sea like old garbage, no friends or loved ones around to mourn." Truth be told, the poor girl's fate struck too close to home after my harrowing escape from a madwoman on the beach only too recently.

"You're right," Sam's eyes had moistened. "I didn't think of that. It makes me more determined to figure out what happened to her and who did it."

"Let's leave these for Alice and her crew to clean. I'm ready to find Landon and see who he thinks might have killed Coco."

"You go ahead," Sam said. "I'll try to catch Alice on her way here and find out the names of the girls who work for her." Sam pulled a slice of Watermelon Pie from the freezer and grinned. "It's time to make a delivery."

~

Griff was waiting for me on the porch of the cabin Sam and I were sharing. He hadn't stuck around for breakfast; he said he didn't want to be in our way.

I unlocked the cabin door and we went inside. Griff stretched his long legs out on the floor and I took the cooler as a seat again.

"They should really have chairs," I said.

"Sure," Griff drew out the word. "They would fit great on the top bunk." He looked pointedly around the miniscule amount of space in the room.

I stuck my tongue out at him.

"Piper," he leaned forward, catching my eye before he continued. "I know things have been really busy and time kind of got away from us, but I want you to know I meant what I said about you. About us."

I wriggled around uncomfortably. Whoops! With a thud my cooler overturned and I was planted hard on the floor.

"Are you okay?" Griff asked. His lips twitched and I narrowed my eyes at his barely contained mirth.

"Chairs!" I grumbled, rubbing my sore hip. "See, we need chairs." Deciding it was best that I stay put on the floor, I crossed my legs and took a deep breath. "Who's Kendra?" I blurted. *Whoops.* That wasn't what I had planned to lead with; really, it wasn't what I planned to say at all actually. I felt heat creep up my neck and into my cheeks.

"What?"

"I'm sorry. I'm sure it isn't any of my business. Sam and I saw you having lunch with some gorgeous girl with a gorgeous yellow dress, and you lied about where you were to Sam and then on the phone your mom yelled something about Kendra looking for you and Sam said Kendra was this wicked smart lawyer or something, I don't remember, anyway then I wondered if she was your lunch date in the yellow dress." I stopped my babbling and shrugged. "So, who's Kendra?" I asked again. It was too late to turn back now.

Griff shook his head slowly back and forth. "Whoa. Okay, first yes Kendra has a legal background, but she decided not to go into law. And yes, she and I met for lunch a few days ago but I didn't lie to Sam. It was work-related. You see...."

A succession of four or five light taps on the door were the only notice we had before Landon ducked in and closed the door behind him.

"You've got to be kidding," Griff sighed.

"Sorry – didn't want to be seen. Am I interrupting?" Landon looked down to meet our stares.

"Yes," Griff said through gritted teeth.

"A little bit," my clipped tone carried the frustration that I was finding difficult to tamp down.

"What are you doing? I thought you were keeping a low profile?"

"I can't just hide in a cabin for the rest of my life. We have to figure this out and I've been thinking," Landon nudged me to scoot over some so he could join our little pow-wow on the floor. "I think I can narrow down who might have killed Coco."

"How?" I asked.

"A timeline."

"A timeline of what?" Griff frowned.

The door flew open and banged into Landon's shoulder before bouncing back.

"Oomph!" This time, the door opened much slower, inching open at a snail's pace as Sam leaned around it holding up a shoe. "Thank gosh," she said. "I thought someone broke in here and hit me with the door. Who did hit me with the door anyway?"

"We really have to get you outfitted with a better weapon than a shoe," I laughed. "At least your last one had a dangerous, pointy heel."

"You hit Landon with the door, Sis. Then it bounced off his thick head and back into you."

Sam looked to Griff, her jaw dropping, then back to Landon. "I'm so, so, so, sorry!"

"It didn't hit me in the head, just the shoulder; your brother's messing with you."

"Come on in and shut the door," I told her.

Landon scooted around so Sam could squeeze in between us and Griff scooted closer to me, away from Landon, and placed a warm hand on my knee. My stomach flip-flopped.

"What did I miss?" Sam asked.

"Landon was about to tell us how he narrowed down the suspects for Coco's murder."

"And who they are, hopefully," Griff added.

"Good." Sam nodded. "After that I'll tell you about the girls working for Alice."

"Alice?" Both men shared a puzzled look.

I waved them off. "Landon, hurry up and tell us. Sam and I still have to go back and make desserts for lunch.

"Yeah, *some of us* are actually working," Sam shot Griff a pointed glance.

I held a hand up between them, like a ref making a call. We didn't have time for that trail of thought. "Landon?" I prompted.

"Okay, here's the deal." He unfolded a sheet of paper with scratches and lines of ink scribbled all across it. "I began to notice a few months ago that the feeling of our assignments started changing."

"Hold on," Griff said. "Can you explain these assignments first. What is it that you or Breaking Chains actually do? I'm trying to understand why you would be in that massage parlor Piper described and still give you the benefit of the doubt, but it doesn't sound like a place where legitimate businesses would go to me."

"Let me give you the summary version: Breaking Chains is mission focused on two things. First, raise awareness of human trafficking. Second, put an end to it. They do this through intervention, outreach, and restoration. Intervention involves prayer teams and data reporting, but that isn't the team I'm with. Restoration is a follow-up service providing housing, education, and resources to women, children, and even men who are able to get out of the trafficking world and that comes later. The part I'm involved with is the second part: outreach. As an outreach team, members get out on the streets, in the cantinas, or other businesses that are suspected of using trafficked victims for business. We hand out cards or gifts to earn trust, often the gifts have a hotline phone number that can be called if they need someone to help them get away from a pimp or boss safely."

"Like the lipstick," Sam said.

"Exactly."

"I had heard about the Thai Massage in one of the online sites where discreet advertisements are often placed. I've been going there on my own for the last two weeks trying to establish trust with some of the girls so I could get more information on who owns it. I'm tired of releasing one fish to have seventeen more scooped up in a net; helping one or two women escape is great but as long as there is a market for sex or cheap labor the demand continues to be met."

"Back to the timeline because speaking of time we are seriously running out of it here," I said as I looked at my phone. "What changed to make you suspicious about your coworkers or teammates?"

"Well," Landon said, "I didn't actually think anything of it at the time, it's just been the last few weeks that I've started to wonder. At the beginning of my career with Breaking Chains, when we participated in the outreach groups, we were talking to fifteen or twenty women a night on the street or five to six in the massage parlors. The few cantinas we went into were eager to sell the *cerveza especial de la casa,* the house special beer, for a premium price which really bought you time with the waitress. After time though, we were able to reach less and less people."

"You don't think it was because you were getting recognized, that maybe word spread on the street that you were slowing down business?" Griff asked, rubbing a hand along the stubble of his jaw. I could tell he wanted to think everything through and be thorough.

"Actually, that is what I thought in the beginning," Landon nodded. "Then it continued even when we went to new places, new cities."

"And you think the establishments had been warned about you?" I asked.

He gave a nod. "I've been going over the teams to find a pattern and I think I finally did."

"Does it narrow the list of people down? Because, so far, all Piper and I have done is managed to grow the list of suspects," Sam pushed red and blonde strands of hair behind her neck.

"Yeah, it does. What I noticed is that six particular people were hired within two weeks of our outreaches going south."

"Six people? That seems like a lot to hire at one time," Sam frowned.

"Breaking Chains underwent a major expansion; these people came onboard during that time."

"Who were they?" I leaned forward across our little circle, trying to see what Landon had written on his timeline sheet.

"Minnie Hitchens, Chaplain Mark Moore, Arthur Cole, Regina Wilson, Jerry Jackson, and August Mitchell."

"I guess we can rule out Arthur from poisoning his own pie," Sam made a checking motion as if eliminating one name from our long list.

"What about of killing Coco?" Griff asked. "We don't actually know which of them was killed first; maybe Arthur killed her and couldn't live with the guilt."

"Urrr," I grumbled and slapped Griff on the leg. "We are trying to make this easier to figure out, not harder!"

He raised his hands and sat back in mock surrender. "Just sayin'."

"I think we've met Chaplain Mark and Regina, unless there are a lot of Regina's you work with?" I waited a second and continued after Landon shook his head in the negative. "That is still a lot of names. Did you narrow it down any further?"

"Slightly. I do think we can eliminate Arthur. Besides being killed himself, he was strictly a business guy and the best business is for Breaking Chains to have a higher tally of individuals helped, not lower. Often contributions are a large part of our operating budget. With no statistics showing we do good then no more contributions would be coming in."

"Down to five," Sam, smile fixed firmly in place as usual, clapped her hands. "Who else can we cross off?"

"To narrow down those five, I started thinking about the places we went that had little to no people around for us to make contact with and who our team consisted of at those times. Those particular missions always involved me and two other team members who have been with me for years, Chaplain Moore, and Regina Wilson."

"But you don't think there is any way it could have been the other two team members? Just because you've known them a long time?"

"No. I don't think it could be them for several reasons. Besides working with them for years before the weird slow down of interventions, one of them had a niece who was a sex trafficking victim and the other retired a month ago."

"Okay, so we're down to you, Chaplain Moore, and Regina Wilson as suspects." Griff ignored the annoyed look I shot him for lumping Landon back into the suspect pool. "Tell us about their roles in the company."

Landon quickly summarized the jobs of the two: Chaplain Moore was one of three chaplains who provided prayer and support for the emotional well-being of both the teams and the victims and joined in on many intervention outreaches; Regina coordinated tips and leads and funneled them into action-plans for intervention missions, assigning them to teams.

"Chaplain Moore is pretty private; he doesn't talk about himself or his past. He only comes into the office to prep and leave on interventions, otherwise we don't really see him." Landon continued, "Regina on the other hand is outspoken, gregarious, well-liked by coworkers, and a workaholic."

"Sam, didn't you say something about your list from Alice?" I asked. "Yikes, and hurry! We have to go make desserts for after lunch."

"Alice said she gets the girls who are on the cleaning crew from a service. She says often she gets new ones every two or three weeks."

"What service?" Griff asked.

"Is that how Coco came out here?" Landon grabbed Sam's arm. "You both said she was working with the cleaning crew when you saw her, right?"

"That's right. Alice couldn't remember the name of the service. Look, Piper is right. We really have to get back to the kitchen," Sam stood followed by Landon. He paced in small, tight strides, rubbing his neck.

Before I finished unfolding my legs from their cramped position, Griff was extending a hand out to me. I took it and he pulled me gently to my feet. "Please, be careful," he whispered against my hair before letting me go and taking a step back.

I nodded. Speech had deserted me again. I decided that was due to being tired and having too much murder on the brain; obviously, it had nothing to do with the proximity of Griff, the warmth I could feel emanating from him, or the tingle of awareness singing my skin where his hand had been. Nope, not that at all.

Before Sam and I got the door open, Landon's pacing stopped short in front of us and he pulled us together into a hug. "Thank you. Thank you for believing me and for your help." With a kiss to my cheek and a squeeze of Sam's shoulder he let us go.

I won't lie – I high-tailed it out of there faster than a barefoot kid on hot asphalt; I could all but feel Griff seething and didn't plan to stick around for the fireworks.

Chapter 22

Sam and I were taking the last Fudge Pie out of the oven when Alice knocked on the back door.

"Hi, Alice," I held the door open. "Come in. Is there something we can do for you?"

The front door banged open and voices trickled our way. Alice's eyes darted through the opening from the kitchen to the dining hall and shook her head with such violence I worried she would get a headache.

"No. No, I can't talk here." Looking past me to Sam she said, "I remembered something. Meet me at your cabin at two-thirty." Turning, Alice scurried off without another word.

"She seemed rattled," I closed the door and looked to Sam who nodded in agreement.

"Much more nervous than when I spoke to her earlier."

"Strange. I guess we have to wait to find out why," I sighed. "And we better get these desserts out to the dessert table before we have a riot on our hands."

I could see that the line had moved quickly through the lunch buffet and was now clogging at the dessert table where we had only set out a plate of Ooey Gooey Butter Cookies and Cinnamon Apple Mini Tarts. Carrying the remaining desserts out on an oversized sheet tray, we placed them on the table to a smattering of applause from those waiting.

Sam played along, first with a bow and then a curtsy that would have impressed the queen. *Seriously, who knows how to curtsy?* Most likely Deidra had included charm school in Sam's childhood somewhere along the way.

"Thank goodness," someone drawled. "We thought something *terrible* might have happened to you."

I scanned the faces, but a crowd was elbowing its way into reach of all the desserts by now and heads bobbed in and out of view. The voice sounded familiar, but I'd only been around these people for a day now. Regardless, I brushed at the chill bumps creeping up my arms. Concern wasn't the emotion I heard laced through the benign words.

~

At a quarter after two, Sam and I were stretched out on our separate bunks waiting for Alice to arrive. Team building activities had resumed for the employees of Breaking Chains. Griff, after much insistence from both of us, had agreed to go back to work. He had several meetings scheduled even though it was a Sunday. Landon went with him to stay off of the police radar.

"Who do you think it might be?" Sam asked aloud.

There wasn't a doubt what she meant. "I'm not sure," I told her. Tracing lines in the bottom of the bunk above my head with my finger, I considered everything we knew. "Alice had opportunity to plant poison in the kitchen, but I can't see a motive. Coco shouldn't have wanted Landon dead if he were trying to help her, but even if she did, how did she get killed herself at the same time? Too bad the sheriff won't share the time of death with us so we could rule her out."

"Yeah, I really think it had to be someone close to Landon and the pie during the blackout."

I smacked myself in the forehead. "I knew I forgot something. Sam, I completely forgot to ask Landon who specifically sat at his table."

A knock, timid and small, sounded at the door.

"That must be Alice," Sam stretched before getting off of her bunk to answer the knock.

I sat up, too. "What's that smell?" I asked wrinkling my nose. It was kind of an acrid, smoky scent. Too late, I saw writhing gray fingers of smoke reaching under the door. "No! Sam don't…"

Sam turned the knob and cried out in pain. I pulled her back as she opened the door and a whoosh of flames licked towards her. Cradling her palm, the flesh rapidly turning fire-engine-red, she kicked the door shut.

"What do we do now?" she cried. "That's the only door. Shouldn't we just try to get through it?"

"And catch our clothes or hair on fire? No, thank you." I looked around. The room was filling fast with smoke. Shouts could be heard outside. *Thank God! Someone noticed the fire.*

"Piper!" Sam's shriek ended in a cough. "We can't stay in here. There's too much smoke."

I dashed to the bathroom and soaked two rags with water. "Here, put this on your mouth and nose," I said handing one to Sam. *Maybe binge-watching Chicago Fire will pay off after all.*

"God, please, please get us out of this cabin," Sam prayed through the rag as tears rolled down her face.

My eyes burned from the smoke and were watering as well. "The window!"

"What?"

"The window; we can go out the window," I pointed to Sam, lowering the rag for a split second so she could understand me.

I knelt to give Sam a boost. I ached for my friend as she gasped in pain, the sharp sill digging into her burnt hand. There was no room to pull a leg over, no chance for a graceful exit. Sam toppled out headfirst and rolled to the side.

My turn. I inhaled through the wet rag and dropped it, holding my breath against the burning in my lungs. I pulled myself up and wriggled my hips through the window. It was a tight squeeze since this tiny cabin came with an equally small window. Sam reached up to me and tugged. We crashed into the ground below and lay there panting. I closed my eyes and breathed in the fresh air.

I heard voices and then felt hands on my elbows. Opening my eyes, I found Chaplain Moore and Roy trying to help Sam and me to our feet.

"Is Alice in there?" Roy's voice shook. "She said she was meeting you two and I can't find her; is she still in there?"

"She wasn't inside," Sam patted Roy's arm reassuringly.

"We never saw her," I told him. Something in the back of my mind bothered me, besides my cabin being set on fire, something small that I couldn't put my finger on.

"Thank heavens and the Almighty for that. Nobody was harmed." Chaplain Moore bowed his head. "We will find your wife," he spoke to Roy.

"Sam's got a pretty bad burn actually," I said.

"Let me see that." Roy turned her wrist over and took in the sight of the angry red skin. "Come on, I'll take you to get this patched up." He led her to the golf cart parked on the trail just a few feet away where he pulled out a first aid kit.

Back on my feet, I walked with Chaplain Moore to the front of the cabin.

"Well, well, well. What do we have here?" Officer Campbell sighted in on me right away. "Burning evidence, Miss Rivers?"

I couldn't respond. My breath caught and my gaze locked onto the charred and blackened front of our cabin. Most of the porch had burnt through, leaving yawning holes. The front wall itself had sustained damage about three-quarters of the way up to the roof but still stood erect.

"Now Officer," Chaplain Moore's voice next to me was startling. I hadn't realized he stayed with me. I turned my face back to the two men.

"I witnessed these young ladies escaping out the back window. You can't possibly think they could have set the fire on the porch and purposefully trapped themselves inside? That's preposterous."

"So, the fire was set?" I asked. I couldn't imagine any other way for it to start, but the thought still disturbed me. "Why did it burn only part of the front? Oh my gosh!" The niggling feeling finally burst through in a complete thought. "Officer Campbell, we heard someone knock on the door right before we saw the smoke. Was anyone hurt?" I glanced on the porch and bent to look under the porch at the ash and debris on the ground.

A small crowd was gathering. "We didn't find anyone out front." Officer Campbell gestured for me to walk with him. "I need to ask you some questions and I'd rather not do it with an audience. You say you heard someone knock?" he asked as we separated ourselves from the group. I watched as Chaplain Moore poked around the burnt areas, moving debris with his shoe, sniffing the wall.

"Mmhmmm," I mumbled. "Officer, shouldn't you stop him from contaminating the scene or something?" I didn't like the idea of one of our top suspects messing around with the evidence from the fire.

"Who? Moore? He's a licensed fire inspector."

"I thought he was the chaplain?"

Officer Campbell just nodded. "He is. He also showed me his license as a fire inspector. Worked for a fire department for years before becoming a chaplain, evidently." Pulling out a notebook, he snapped his fingers at me. "Back to my questions."

Chapter 23

"You mean Officer Grumpy thinks that whoever knocked on the door set the fire?" Sam asked.

"Yep," I sipped my lemonade and leaned forward to rest my elbows on the cold work island in the kitchen of the dining cabin. We had one more round of desserts to make, a killer to catch, and no cabin to call home-away-from-home for the rest of the day. "Though I think he was disappointed he couldn't pin this on me somehow."

"That reminds me! Griff was going to talk to Mother and see if she knew what was in that little black canister. Call him and let's see."

"Right now?" I asked. "Oh no!" I rolled my eyes upward. "I completely forgot to tell you that I slipped up and asked Griff who Kendra was."

"What did he say?"

"He didn't get to…we were interrupted…by Landon!" I snorted remembering the look on Griff's face.

"No, he didn't!" Sam slapped the table. At my nod she burst into laughter but sobered quickly. "Uh-oh. Maybe it wasn't a good idea to leave them alone."

I finished my lemonade and put the glass in the sink. "You want to walk the beach? I think better when I'm moving. I can call Griff while we walk."

"Yep, let's go."

"Hello?" Griff answered on the first ring.

"Hey," I said. "Sam's with me; I have you on speaker. She said you were going to see if

Deidra knew what was in the canister that the police used as cause to arrest me."

"Yep. She knew. Piper, I have to tell you something though. You know my mother never does a favor for free."

I gulped.

"Do you have to go to the country club dinner, too?" Sam leaned over my phone to ask.

"Worse."

"Why do you people always say worse?" My voice rose an octave as bad feelings unfurled inside of me. "Just tell us, what did your mother require of you?"

"That I escort Kendra to the Independence Day Parade."

"Good grief!" Sam's eyes rolled upward. "The woman is diabolical."

I heard Landon in the background over Griff's phone saying, "I have really got to meet this woman. The way y'all talk about her, I keep getting flashes of Cruella Deville."

I snickered. He had a point, though Deidra would rather be dead than have any white in her hair.

"I'm sorry, Piper. This doesn't change a thing for us, I promise." Griff's voice rumbled low.

I swallowed. It could have been worse; I had fully expected Deidra to tell Griff to stay away from me, but I guess the woman knew she had a few limits after all. "It's fine; it's done," I snapped. "Tell us what the canister contained."

"Cyanide. Arthur Cole was poisoned and the cyanide in the container is a match to what was found on the Peanut Butter Pie and in Arthur Cole's system."

"But I'd never seen that container before in my life!"

"That's the only thing keeping you out of jail right now, besides mother of course; there were none of your prints found on the container. In fact, there were no fingerprints whatsoever."

"Still, if that cyanide was used by the murderer, then someone is actively trying to set me up." I shook my head. "Landon, I forgot to ask you, who all sat at your table that could have easily reached the pie with the cyanide?"

"Let me think." A few seconds of dead air passed before he startled. "Two of the people on my suspect list timeline sat at that table. I can't believe I didn't realize it before!"

"Who?" Sam grabbed my wrist and pulled it and my phone closer, listening closely for the names.

"Both Chaplain Moore and Regina sat at the table with us."

Sam gasped. "Piper, are you sure we should stay here instead of going home? The police can figure this out. With the canister and then the cabin fire, plus Chaplain Moore poking around the burnt areas – it's just getting really dangerous, you know?"

"What cabin fire?" Griff asked.

By the time we hung up the phone, Griff and Landon were demanding we leave and go home. Landon apologized for getting us involved and told us to forget all of it.

"Let me guess, they're on the way here?" Sam asked after I gave the guys our answer. No way were we leaving. Our catering contract wasn't up, plus we had to be close if we were making the killer this nervous.

"Yeah. It'll be a miracle if Griff doesn't get multiple speeding tickets heading back out here. I figure we have two, maybe three, hours max before they show up beating their chests and trying to drag us away." I rolled my eyes and grinned. The mental image of Griff as Tarzan wasn't too bad.

"Talking about the fire reminded me: I sure hope Roy finds Alice." Sam interrupted my daydreaming. "I'm worried about her," she chewed on her bottom lip. "What if, on her way to see us, Alice saw whoever set the fire and they took her?"

"Maybe we should go visit Roy and see if he's had any news." I looked at my phone. "We still have forty-five minutes before we need to start baking anyway."

We turned back to the direction we had come from. The wind, no longer at our backs, whipped sand and salty spray into our faces. I shielded my eyes. "I hope there isn't another storm coming this weekend."

"The skies look clear all around," Sam scanned the horizon. "I don't think I can take any more excitement of any kind either."

Mere minutes of walking brought us to the larger cabin that Roy and Alice shared on the property. We had seen his golf cart parked there in passing several times, as the cabin was near the main entrance.

"His golf cart is here," I pointed. "Maybe Alice is home with him; I think I hear voices."

The voices grew louder, raised in shouting. Sam cringed. "Maybe we should come back later?"

I stood, hesitating, I really wanted to be sure Alice was okay. At the same time, if they were fighting, they probably would be embarrassed to have an audience.

All of a sudden, the voices stopped. The door of the cabin was thrown open and it was too late to leave. Sam and I gasped. Alice was not the woman who appeared in the doorway.

"Hello!" Regina's smile stretched wide. "I was just visiting with Roy here about how to fix a leaky faucet. Are you having problems, too?"

"Nope," Sam squeaked.

Regina narrowed her eyes. Grasping at straws for a plausible reason to be at the maintenance man's cabin, I blurted, "We just came to see if Alice wanted anymore Watermelon Pie."

"Oh? I'd love to try some of that."

"We don't have it right now. We were checking in so we knew how much to make."

"Pity." Regina sniffed. "I've got to run. Roy, thank you for your help. I really hate leaky faucets."

Roy remained silent, only nodding from the doorway and not quite meeting Regina's gaze.

"We don't need anymore pie," Roy said to us as we attempted to squeeze our way inside. The door shut in our faces and I swear Regina smirked.

"I guess I didn't miss out on anything fabulous after all. Watermelon in a pie does sound strange." Regina smiled and waved. "Bye ladies."

Chapter 24

"I wonder where Landon and Griff are," Sam mused as she licked the last bit of chocolate off her fingers.

Our arrival back at the dining cabin had interrupted the cleaning crew; Alice had not been among them. By now, the dinner crowd had come and gone and there had been no sign of the guys.

"I really expected them back by now," I agreed. Sam and I sat in lounge chairs up amongst the dunes, staring at the ocean as the sun began its descent toward the waves.

"Did you try calling them?"

"Yes. Straight to voicemail on both phones."

"Maybe they stopped for gas. Or to eat." Sam tossed out options but we both knew it didn't feel right.

"Come on," I stood up and grabbed my flip flops from beside the chair, holding onto them as I marched back through the cluster of cabins and up the trail.

Sam, God bless her, didn't even hesitate. After keeping stride with my determined pace in silence, she finally asked. "You want to tell me where we're going in such a hurry?"

I slowed and she took the opportunity to slide her shoes onto her feet. "We are going to talk to Alice. She has to be home by now, surely."

Knock, knock, knock.

Nothing. No answer.

"There's a light on inside," Sam stood on tiptoe and tried to peer through the gingham curtains.

Bang. Bang. Bang. I beat on the door harder. *Come on Roy, Alice, open up.* The knot of worry in my stomach was expanding like bread left to rise.

At last, the door opened and Roy hustled us inside. Locking and sliding the bolt behind us, he glanced out the curtained window before turning to us.

"What do you think you're doing here?" he demanded in a whisper. "Haven't you caused enough trouble?" Gone was the kind tour guide we met yesterday morning. Roy was angry. His hands shook.

"Roy, we need to talk to Alice."

"Is she here?" Sam added, looking around.

Following Sam's gaze, I took stock of the cabin's interior. A haphazard stack of dishes filled the sink. How they hadn't toppled over already I couldn't guess. Dirt and sand dotted the floors. Either the woman in charge of the cleaning crew didn't believe in bringing work home with her, or she hadn't been back home this afternoon.

"Roy. Where's Alice?" I asked again.

His face crumpling, Roy stumbled to the well-worn couch and sat down, burying his face in his hands. "I don't know," came his muffled reply.

"What?"

We moved closer to Roy and Sam took the seat next to him. After scooting down a plethora of magazines and knickknacks, I perched on the coffee table directly in front of Roy.

Reaching out a hand to his arm, I said in a quiet but firm voice, "Roy, you have to tell us what is going on. Who has who? Is Alice okay? We never heard from her after she was supposed to meet us. We want to help."

"You can't help." His shoulders shook as he took a deep breath. "Alice is in danger if I tell anyone."

"Who is she in danger from?" Sam's eyes grew alarmed. "Roy, who has Alice. Is she okay?"

"Who threatened you? If you tell us, we can try to help."

He pulled away and shook his head. "I can't."

I decided to try a different tactic. Pulling out my phone, my fingers sped over the keys until I found what I wanted. Turning the screen to Roy, I showed him the first photo. "Was it this man?" I bit my lip, waiting.

Roy's response surprised me; I had been so sure. "No," he said matter-of-factly.

Disappointed but determined, I closed the profile picture of Chaplain Moore and scrolled through Breaking Chains' website until I found the next photo. "Was it her?" I asked, flipping the phone back to face Roy.

This time he didn't speak; he didn't need to. Roy flinched backwards and color drained from his face.

"Roy," Sam spoke, "Regina wasn't here to talk about leaky plumbing today, was she?"

"No. That woman came here furious, wanting to know if Alice had told me what she wanted to talk to you two about today."

"Did she?" I leaned forward.

"No. No, she didn't tell me a blasted thing, though I tried to get her to. Alice has been nervous all weekend though, ever since that poor man died."

"That's understandable," Sam said. "Death makes many people uncomfortable; murder is even more frightening to consider."

"Back to Regina," I licked my lips. "Roy, did she say where Alice is at?"

Shoulders slumping, Roy swiped at a tear on wrinkled cheek. "No. She just said that if I wanted Alice back, I better keep my mouth shut. Leaky faucets, she said, get plugged."

"We have to go to the police," Sam didn't get the words from her mouth before Roy jerked violently.

"No!" He stood and glared at us. "Don't you dare. I don't know how you figured things out about Regina, but don't you dare tell the police and put my Alice in danger. Get out. Get out!" He waved his hands at us and advanced.

Sam nearly overturned the coffee table in her haste to get away from the shouting maintenance man. We hurried from the cabin and down the trail, at last stopping to catch our breath on a small bench.

"How did you know?"

"Huh?" I leaned back on the bench, my mind reeling.

"How did you know it was Regina? We had so many suspects."

"I didn't know. I honestly thought Chaplain Moore to be the guilty party. He sat at the table where Arthur Cole died, he was present at the beach when Coco's body was found. Heck, he dug all around our porch and I just knew he must be burying evidence."

"Then why Regina?"

"When Roy had no visible response to Chaplain Moore, I tried Regina because she had been at the cabin earlier and it felt odd. Plus, she and Moore were both around right before the police searched the grocery bag and found the poison."

"You think Regina dropped it?"

"She either dropped it or put it in my bag on purpose."

"Wow. What now?" Sam fiddled with the hem of her t-shirt.

"Now we find Griff and Landon," I stood and stretched. "Maybe they are back and went to the dining cabin."

A trip to the dining cabin proved fruitless, as did a walk to the cabin the guys had shared last night.

"Nobody is here," Sam said as I pounded on the door for the third time.

"Let's call them."

"You'll have to. I let my battery die so I wouldn't have to get any more texts from Mother with prospective date photos for the dinner."

Leaning against the cabin door, I punched call beside Griff's contact picture, a photo I had snapped of him biting into a giant cookie.

"Hello," a feminine voice cackled. "I just knew you would call. Listen carefully."

Chapter 25

"Who is this?" I snapped. The hairs on the back of my neck stood as the speaker laughed the answer back at me.

"It's Regina," I hissed to Sam in a whisper, covering the mouthpiece. Sam leaned her head against mine to listen.

"Regina, where is Griff? And Alice?"

"I'll ask the questions here," Regina barked over the phone. "What did Alice tell you?"

"Nothing. We never got to speak with her. Did you set the cabin fire?"

"Aren't you a smart little cookie; if you keep your mouth shut, then nobody has to get hurt."

I could feel my blood boiling. "Nobody else, you mean? Last time that I checked, two people are dead."

"And isn't that unfortunate. Unless you want it to be your boyfriends here, you'll do as I say."

She must have Landon too, I realized.

Sam grasped my hand and I squeezed back. "What do you want, Regina?" I asked.

"I want you to go bake your crummy desserts tonight and act normal. Don't go poking your nose where it doesn't belong. Tomorrow, I'll send instructions where you can find your friends and that idiot cleaning woman with the big mouth." Regina hung up without waiting for a response.

I tried calling again but got an error message. "She must have turned the phone off," I told Sam.

"If she is going to release Griff, Landon, and Alice tomorrow, then that must mean she has a way out tonight. She is planning on getting away with the murders."

"Come on. We have to go bake."

"What?!" Sam's jaw dropped and she looked at me like I had lost my mind.

"You heard Regina. She specifically said we have to make desserts and pretend things are fine. What if she has someone here watching us? Or she shows up herself? We don't want to put the guys in more danger if we can prevent it."

"Urghh." Sam growled and stood. Stomping off down the path she called over her shoulder, "This is stupid you know. Stupid. We have to do something about this and for once cookies are not the answer."

~

I sprinkled the last few lines of blue sanding sugar onto the plates, arcing it up and down to give the appearance of waves. "Are the Mini Seashell Cakes ready to be plated?" I asked Sam without looking up from my work. We had gone to the kitchen to bake, as instructed. I wouldn't risk going against Regina; the outcome for Griff and Landon was too unpredictable.

A long pause filled the air before finally she answered, but not as I expected. "I'm really worried."

"About the cakes?"

"No. About Griff and Landon. Alice too for that matter."

"I'm thinking of a plan. First, we have to get through dessert tonight. Are the cakes ready?"

"Yes," Sam grumbled. She brought over a tray of cooled and frosted cupcake-sized personal cakes, each decorated to look like a seashell.

These would be our star dessert tonight. *They have to be just perfect.* I arranged and re-arranged the Mini Seashell Cakes up on the platter to appear as if the waves washed them to shore.

"What exactly is the plan?" Sam asked.

"Pray."

Sam nodded and did just that. Whispering, she began. "Father in heaven, we don't know what to do or where to find our friends. Please help us; please protect Griff, Landon, and Alice. Please help us find them."

~

Regina did not show up for dinner or dessert at the wellness retreat that evening as far as Sam and I could tell. I peeked around the doorframe once more. "I still don't see her."

"Do you think she already fled the area?"

"I don't know, maybe. Are you ready to go?" We skipped dinner; neither of us had an appetite for eating.

Sam nodded and removed her apron, hanging it over a stool. "Yeah. Tell me, where are we going? And please, please say the police station."

"Well, not the police station, but maybe the police," I told her in a low voice. "Come on," I motioned that she should follow me out through the back door.

Outside I glanced around. We appeared to be alone; not a soul meandered down the trail, the porch rockers sat empty and still. "We can't go to the police station. That would attract too much attention and people might not believe us. But, if we can find Officer Grumpy, we can talk to him. I've already been arrested so a follow-up from the police wouldn't be out of the ordinary. He's got to be around here somewhere."

"Okay. Split up or stick together?"

"It would be faster to split up…but honestly I think we should stay together. Every bad thing that ever happens in a scary movie happens when the group goes separate ways."

With a serious expression and not a single sarcastic remark about TV not being real life, Sam nodded. "That's true. Together it is."

We scoured the whole resort from the beach to the main office. I kicked at loose pebbles in the parking lot by the office. "Of course! Of all the times for Officer Grumpy to make himself scarce, he picks today. Any other moment he'd be popping out of the bushes trying to arrest me, but now he's vanished."

"Here," Sam handed me a business card she had swiped off the front desk. "Call him."

Sure enough, Officer Campbell's name and cell were printed neatly in front of me. I dialed. And waited. The phone rang and rang but, in the end, went straight to voicemail. "Officer Gr..uh..Campbell, this is Piper Rivers. Please give me a call the moment you get this." Rattling off my cell number, I hung up.

"Now do we go to the police station?" Sam begged, tugging at the hem of her t-shirt and looking around. Sam never fidgeted. Her actions told me better than words how scared she felt and I couldn't blame her. *Oh God, please don't let anything happen to Griff, to any of them.*

"Let's try one more place," I said. Grabbing Sam by the arm, I towed her with me and sprinted to my truck.

"What are you doing? Your keys are in your bag at Griff's cabin, aren't they? We're going the wrong way."

Letting go of Sam's arm, I crouched on my knees by the driver's door and leaned as far as I could underneath my truck. "Tada!" I extricated myself and held up a single key with a grin.

Sam rubbed the sides of her head and shook it at me. "This is because you lose your keys so often, isn't it?"

"Hush. Get in the truck." I stuck my tongue out at her and moved to unlock the door. I revved the engine and threw it in drive before Sam even buckled her seatbelt.

"I would ask where we are going again," Sam said, after the buckle to her seatbelt clicked into place "but I'm afraid I already know."

"It's the only other place we might get information."

Sam groaned.

Chapter 26

I parked on the far side of the Dollar Store parking lot, below a light pole with darkened, shot out bulbs. Gathering storm clouds had darkened the evening sky faster than expected. The darkness could be a foreboding sign, or a blessing of concealment; I chose to be thankful for the concealment. We sat in silence, but not the companionable sort. More like the terrified, barely breathing, afraid to talk, not daring to move sort.

"Now what?" Sam finally whispered.

I shrugged. "I thought we would wait a bit and watch the door. If Regina comes out, we call 911 and report a robbery, or kidnapping, or car theft – whichever we can get them to respond to, I don't care which."

"That's it?" I could hear the surprise in my friend's voice. I hated to disappoint her.

"Not quite," I squeaked.

"What if Regina doesn't come out?"

"That's the part you aren't going to like."

"Piper…"

"If Regina doesn't come out, then we go in. Maybe BeeBee thought of something else to tell us or can point us in another direction to look." I glanced over at her in the dim interior. "It's the best I can think of; we have to get them back."

"I know," she sighed.

We returned to our silent vigil. For ten minutes there wasn't a single movement outside other than trash blowing across parking lots as the wind picked up speed.

BAM!

The door to the Thai Massage Parlor opened and the wind ripped it from the small hand holding it, banging the door into the wall.

"Is that…" Sam leaned forward.

"No. It's the one they called Mamasan." I recognized the petite Asian women we met on our previous visit. "If she's leaving, there is a chance we can sneak in and talk to BeeBee."

We watched as Mamasan shuffled across the parking lot and into the vape shop on the other side of the massage parlor.

Waiting no longer than it took for the shop door to close, I scrambled out of the truck and sprinted for Thai Massage. I heard Sam's door shut and felt her catch up to me.

"Glad you brought sensible shoes on this trip," I teased. She wore sneakers and it was in fact only one of about four times I'd seen her in something flat. She even wore heels at the bakery most days. "What made you wear those today?"

"I had a bad feeling. Remind me that trips with you are a bad idea in any footwear," she retorted in a whisper as we crept near the door. With a glance behind us, I turned the knob. "Thank God. It's unlocked."

"That might not be a good thing," Sam whispered. "It might mean she's coming right back."

"Then we better hurry."

We eased inside the building and closed the door inch by inch to avoid making noise. The fluorescent lights were all turned off; only a few lamps lit the hallway. When nobody came to greet us, I exhaled a sigh of relief. The small foyer sat empty, unless you counted the layers of lingering grime and dirt from cigarettes and who knows what – those were thick enough to pull up their own chair.

"Look," Sam pointed to a framed certificate on the wall to our left. "This health inspection is from six years ago."

Unsurprised, I shook my head. Creeping down the hall, we made our way to the door where our visit with BeeBee had taken place yesterday. At least, we tried to creep. I bumped into a side table and Sam nearly knocked a mirror down as she flattened herself up against the wall.

"What are you doing?" I whispered.

"Trying not to be seen," she hissed.

I rolled my eyes, a gesture she missed in the dark of course. "You aren't a chameleon!"

Sure enough, our stealth mode wasn't at all effective. A throat cleared and we both jumped. *Not Regina, please not Regina* I prayed silently.

"Piper? Sam?" the voice sounded small, shaky.

I turned and looked at the young woman approaching us. "BeeBee!"

"Thank God," Sam slumped on the wall, clutching at her chest. "You gave me a heart attack, a mini one maybe, but I'm certain it stopped for a second."

"What are you doing here?" BeeBee asked.

"It is a really long story. Have you seen this woman?" I flicked my phone to life, the bright screen temporarily blinding me, then scrolled to my screenshots. Holding up the headshot of Regina, I watched BeeBee's face. A flash of recognition lit her eyes, then confusion furrowed her brows.

"She has come in a few times. Only to talk to Mamasan and she never stays long. I saw her here today."

"Really?" Sam stood up, excited.

"We need to know anything you know about her," I said. A rattling sound at the door halted anything BeeBee might have said.

"Quick," she pushed us into a side room and eased the door partially shut. "Shhh." She held her index finger to her lips and waved us to the corner. We listened, barely daring to breathe, as the front door opened and closed followed by footsteps tapping across the floor. An eternity later, we heard another door close.

BeeBee peered out. "You have to leave." She huddled next to us and whispered, "I don't know what happened but Mamasan is very angry today and that woman whose photo you showed me, she showed up in a rage this afternoon. Bad business is going down, I just know it. You can't be found here and especially not with me."

"Please, BeeBee," Sam reached out to her but BeeBee jerked back.

"No. I don't want to end up like Coco. I can't help you, I'm sorry."

"Landon is missing," I told her. Hope flared inside me as she paused.

"That is very sad, but there is nothing I can do to help." She shook her head and my little flame of hope whooshed out. "I will make sure the coast is clear. You leave. In one minute, you go." With that she whisked into the hall and left no time for argument.

I kept time on my watch. At the one-minute mark, I placed a hand on Sam's shoulder. "We have to go."

Without a word, she tiptoed to the door and flattened herself against the wall again. I bit my lip to keep from laughing. *That's it, no more spy movies* I resolved. Rather than wait for 007 to peek out the door with only her eyes six more times, I moved past her and opened it wide. Muted voices could be heard behind one of the doors, though I couldn't tell which.

Waving Sam behind me, I slipped into the hall. My footsteps rang in my ears like thunderclaps and I froze. The voices continued. Taking to tiptoe again, we were halfway down the hall when I started to breathe normally again. *We're going to make it.* Elation and adrenaline coursed through me, followed by crashing disappointment. *I guess we have to go to the police after all.* I squeezed my eyes shut against the tears that threatened. I had been so hopeful we could get a lead or find Regina and convince her to release the guys.

I pushed back the negative thoughts and feelings. Not much further and we would be out. Then, all hell broke loose.

Chapter 27

Dory from Finding Nemo chose that moment to shout "Eh Mr. Grumpy Gills. Eh Mr. Grumpy Gills" over and over. Okay, maybe it wasn't Dory in the fins so to speak; rather, that was the ringtone that I set up for Officer Grumpy. It played on a loop from my phone. Loud. That man has to have the worst timing ever.

"Crap. Crap!" I fumbled to silence the phone but dropped it. Too late, our presence had been announced. Mamasan, BeeBee, and a lithe Asian man, a bit taller than them and bare shoulders covered in tattoos of some kind of demon mask, came bursting from a back room. Sam and I sprinted for the door.

"Ow!" Sam yelped behind me.

I looked back and sucked in my breath. Looked forward. Only a foot from the door. So close, yet so far.

"Let her go," I raised my hands in surrender. "We were just leaving. Sorry, we didn't realize you were closed."

The man retained a tight grip on Sam.

Behind Mamasan, BeeBee's eyes bulged wide in fear and her lower lip trembled.

With soft, graceful movements, Mamasan glided forward and bent to pick up my traitorous phone from the tile floor.

"You had phone call, yes? Let's see who."

I groaned inwardly.

"The police?" Mamasan looked up, eyes narrowing, gaze sharp. "Who are you? Why the police call?"

"I'm nobody; don't worry," I tried. It was useless. She had dismissed me already, no longer listening.

"Asnee, take them to the back," she instructed her deadly looking muscle. "Tie them up." Turning, she pocketed my phone and shoved past BeeBee on her way to the front office.

Sam wriggled and I lashed out at the man's face as he reached for me. His grip on her didn't loosen.

Out of the corner of my eye, I saw movement as I dodged his hand again. BeeBee screeched and leapt onto his back. My jaw dropped. I kicked out at him, but on connecting with his solid, muscular legs, I only managed to hurt my foot and earn a scowl.

Asnee pivoted backward and slammed BeeBee into the wall. The girl crumpled to the floor unconscious.

Mamasan, inserting herself into the melee with force, wrenched my arm back and pierced the skin above my elbow with her dagger-sharp nails. "Bring that one," she tossed her head at BeeBee and proceeded to lead the way down the hall. I followed without resistance. Now had proven not to be the time for escape.

Asnee lifted BeeBee around the waste and carried her like a limp sack in the crook of one arm. I prayed the girl would be okay. I didn't glimpse any blood.

We were hustled down the hall and jerked to a stop in front of the third locked door. Mamasan let go of my arm to fish a key out of a deep pocket, the pocket that had swallowed my phone up, but it wasn't like I had anywhere to go with Asnee assuming a wide-legged pose and blocking the path to freedom.

I looked at Sam; fear etched lines into her face, but the clench of her jaw gave me hope. She was calculating, thinking, she hadn't given up. I nodded at her and she nodded back. A silent exchange, but deeply understood regardless. We might be caught, but we would get out of this and we would do it together.

Mamason unclipped the heavy padlock from the bolt on the door and swung it inward. My eyes widened. Heart leaping to my throat, I drank in the sight of Griff. Next, I saw Landon and even Alice. All three sat on the floor, zip-tied. Cloth wound around their mouths, holding them silent.

Alice shrank back in fear as Mamasan pointed me into the room, but the expressions on the faces of Griff and Landon didn't waver; fury emanated from them. Griff met Asnee stare for stare, with hard eyes narrowed, growling as Sam was shoved into the corner by Alice.

Sam and I were fitted with matching accessories, bound tight hand and foot. As Mamasan leaned near to gag me, I head-butted her. She returned the favor with a sharp backhand; the stinging lip was well worth it because, while she stood and rubbed her head, I scooted close to Sam and mouthed *knife in my pocket.* She gave me a sharp nod then looked away.

After Mamasan and Asnee finished trussing us up like Thanksgiving Day turkeys, they bound BeeBee's hands in front of her, flipped the light switch off, and left. I heard the bolt slide into place and the clamp of the lock being put back on.

Sitting very still, we all listened. My eyes adjusted to the dim room, not pitch black thanks to the sliver of light trickling around the edges of the door from the hall, but I dared not move until Mamasan and Asnee were definitely gone.

After long minutes with only the sound of Alice sniffling, I scooted to Sam. She spun around backward to me and I maneuvered the leg with the pocket at my knee containing the knife up against her hands. *Thank goodness I don't button these cargo pockets –* the thought whizzed through my head as seconds drew out and Sam painstakingly fumbled around until, at last, she was able to grab the knife. For a moment, it felt like her bound hands were going to be stuck in the pocket, her fists too big to withdraw. Determined, she yanked free. *Now, what to do with the knife?* I tried to picture Sam opening it behind her back and cutting the zip tie and gulped behind the gag, images of bloody fingers coming to mind.

I felt Sam shift away from me and could just make out her shape scooting away in the dim light. Smart, Sam! She scooted right up to Griff and, I assumed, plopped the knife into his fingers.

Snap!

The waiting was torturous, but at last the pluck of plastic giving way sounded and Griff was moving fast. With a flick of his wrist, he severed the plastic from his feet and shuffled to the light switch. After a few swipes of his hand on the wall, he found it and light glared down at us again.

Griff knelt and carefully cut Sam loose and then me. Helping me to my feet, Griff squeezed my hands; leaning his forehead against mine, he whispered. "Do you have to keep getting kidnapped?"

I smiled wide. "Just following your lead."

"Griff," Sam said, swatting at her brother. "You have to cut Landon loose."

"Do I?"

I shook my head at the grin steeling over his face.

"Yes." Sam crossed her arms and pursed her lips at him.

I dropped to my knees beside BeeBee, cradling her head, as Griff freed both Landon and a sobbing Alice. Sam knelt with Alice, trying to quieten her before we were discovered.

I shook BeeBee gently. Stirring, her eyes opened and her mouth widened as if she were going to scream. With her knocked out, Asnee hadn't bound her feet or gagged her.

"Shh." I put a finger to my lips. "It's okay. Griff is going to cut you loose." I nodded at him.

With slow hands, he showed her the knife. At her nod, Griff knelt and cut the band from BeeBee's wrists. She rubbed the back of her head and winced in pain.

"You have a knot," I told her. "We need to get you to a hospital to check for a concussion or bleeding. Are you okay?"

"A little dizzy," she admitted. "I'll live."

I helped her slide over to sit beside Alice and she took over comforting the frightened woman.

Sam, Landon, Griff and I huddled together to form a plan.

"What do we have to use as a weapon besides Piper's knife?" Landon asked.

"Weapons!"

"Shush!" I put a hand over Sam's mouth.

At the raised eyebrow, I removed it.

"Weapons? I don't want to hurt anyone," Sam whispered.

"Listen, we don't know if they have more people coming or not." Griff looked at each of us. "If we are doing this, it has to be now. Landon and I can break down the door, but it is going to cause a lot of noise."

Landon nodded. "They'll be ready for us. Just because we haven't seen a gun doesn't mean they don't have one handy. You two stay back until we're sure. Then, if you get the chance, take down Mamasan. Griff and I will stop Asnee."

"Is this where we put our hands in and yell break?" I asked. BeeBee snorted in the corner.

Sam pinched me and I smothered a laugh. "What? I wasn't the cheerleader or the football player; I don't know how these team things work."

"You need your head checked," Sam rolled her eyes at me and huffed.

Clearly, we handle high stress situations differently. I took her hand and squeezed. "We are almost out of here. We can do this."

"What makes you so sure?" she asked.

"Because I'm hungry," I answered with a shrug. "You know nothing gets in the way of food for me."

"Oh, boy. Step back Griff, Landon. You might as well let Piper break down the door. She nearly removed an indecisive four-year-old from the ice cream parlor once for taking too much time in line before us; she's a menace."

She said it with all the sarcasm she could muster, but Sam still smiled at me. I could see her relaxing and getting ready for what had to be done.

Crash!

Thud-thud-thud.

Chapter 28

We jumped. The noise came from somewhere else in the building; not a single one of us had moved a muscle.

"What in the world?" Scenarios of the building being torn down around us or men on the way to kill us flitted through my brain. I had no idea how to reconcile the sudden burst of sound into our quiet captivity.

Alice shook and sobbed in full now, loud wailing cries mixed with pleas for forgiveness.

BeeBee, giving up on her task of calming the woman, came and huddled between Sam and Landon.

The noises drew closer. Shouting voices could be heard, but no words distinguished.

"Help!" Alice screamed; a shrill, desperate screech. Sam ran back to her and tried to hush the yells. "Hellllp!" Alice continued.

Pounding footsteps made their way to our door. It shook.

"Break this lock!" someone demanded from the hallway.

Griff and Landon squared their feet, arms up, bracing for a fight while I tugged BeeBee backward from the door. We had no idea who would be coming through it.

Violent banging commenced. The lock gave way and the door crashed open.

Hands dropping to their sides, Griff and Landon relaxed their posture.

I peered around them and relief coursed through me. "Officer Campbell!"

"How did you find us?" Sam exclaimed.

"Everybody okay in here?" Officer Campbell asked before his eyes lit on Landon. "You."

"I can explain," Landon lifted his palms up as he stepped up to the officer. "I didn't hurt Arthur or Coco."

"You left the site when everyone was explicitly ordered to stay put. Because of you, my men have been on a wild goose chase."

"I only needed to find some answers." Landon held his hands.

"Finding answers is my job," Officer Campbell growled. "You're going to have to come back to the station."

"Officer Campbell," I interrupted. "BeeBee needs to go to a hospital."

"And Regina, you have to catch Regina. She's behind all of this." Sam waved her arms, her lips a tight line of anger instead of her typical carefree smile.

"Quiet!" Officer Campbell yelled. Silence fell, interrupted by each hiccupped-breath Alice let out, her sobs finally subsiding.

"First, EMTs are on their way for this young lady," he pointed to BeeBee. "After that, we are all going to take a trip to the station where I will get each of your statements and sort this mess out. Regina Wilson has been picked up based on a tip," he eyed the group and Landon shuffled his feet. "So far, we have no evidence to hold her. I'm still unclear what role each of you had to play and none of this changes the fact that the poison, the murder weapon itself, made an appearance in the possession of you, Miss Rivers."

"But I was kidnapped!" *Surely, we can't still be back to this.* "I didn't lock myself up in here."

Officer Campbell narrowed his eyes at me. Then, ignoring us, he shouted orders at nearby deputies to escort us to the vehicles outside and on to the police station.

"Look on the bright side, Piper," Griff whispered as we trudged down the hall. "Maybe down at the jail you'll get a frequent visitor prize."

"Ha-ha-ha," I stuck my tongue out at him.

Outside, rain drizzled down. Through the drops pelting the windows of one police cruiser, I could see Mamasan handcuffed in the back seat. Whether or not Asnee had been captured, I couldn't tell.

BeeBee as well as Alice were led to an ambulance. The doors closed behind them and the vehicle sped off.

Leading the rest of us to dark SUVs, the deputies helped us inside and slammed the door. We were not, I can happily report, handcuffed or under arrest at this point.

"It could be worse," Sam said, reading my mind.

Out the window, lights could be seen flipping on throughout the Thai Massage Parlor. Police clearly were continuing their search of the building. I turned to better face the others. "Since we have time, why don't one of you explain how you got kidnapped." I grinned at Griff and Landon, crossing my arms. Bound to be an interesting story, I couldn't wait to hear it.

"Yeah, the last time we heard, you were on your way to check up on us." Sam raised her eyebrows.

"We can't save the interrogation for the police?" Griff asked, a wry grin teasing at the corner of his mouth.

"Nope." Shaking my head, I looked between the two. "Who wants to start?"

Landon stretched both arms out in front of him, cracking his knuckles. "First off, I might have called in an anonymous tip to Officer Campbell about Chaplain Moore and Regina. I still wasn't sure who murdered Arthur or why, but I needed the police looking for someone besides me while we investigated."

"And we actually did come back to the retreat," Griff added. "Right as we pulled up, Regina tore out of the parking lot like a madwoman. Landon insisted we follow her. I planned to call you and tell you where we ended up, but things happened too fast."

Glancing out the window, I watched the police carry cardboard boxes, draped protectively with plastic, and put them in the trunk of the cruiser. Curious as to what they found but knowing Officer Grumpy would be unlikely to share, I turned back to listen to the guys' tale.

"Regina rushed straight back to the massage parlor. I decided to go in and confront her, find out what business she had there; Griff agreed to come in as backup." Landon rubbed his neck. "We could hear yelling as soon as we got inside. I found Regina screaming at Alice about keeping her mouth shut. I tried to stop her, but when Regina turned around, I saw she had a gun."

"Unlike Landon, I didn't rush in. Two of Regina's thugs caught me in the hall before I could call anybody. I managed to take one of them down but the other had some kind of insane martial arts moves; he tripped me and then Regina held the gun on both Landon and I while we were bound."

I had difficulty picturing someone taking down Griff, but having seen Asnee in person I would guess he had the skills to pull it off.

"That must have been where Regina went after we saw her leave Roy's cabin," Sam said.

"Yes," I agreed. "She already had Alice and came to check her bases, make sure nobody else knew whatever Alice wanted to tell us."

"I think I know what that was," Landon said.

"Oh?"

"Yes. Alice was a wreck. She kept swearing to Regina that she didn't tell anyone about getting the girls from her. You two said Coco came into the kitchen with the cleaning ladies yesterday morning?" At Sam's nod, Landon continued. "I think Regina operated multiple trafficking rings – sex and labor – and that she supplied Alice with girls to work for next to nothing."

"How in the world would Alice get mixed up in that?" I wondered.

"Who knows," he shrugged.

Griff spoke up, "What I want to know is how you two found us?"

"On accident," I shrugged.

Sam snorted. "Yes, Piper's genius plan to get information that actually ended up getting us captured."

We explained about talking to Roy and worrying about putting Alice in danger by going to the police, the phone call to Griff's phone, and our actions from there.

"Oh my gosh!" I sat bolt upright and clapped my hands over my mouth. "My phone!"

"I'm sure we can get your phone later," Sam said.

"No, you don't understand. I've got to find that phone now." Leaping from the car, I ran across the parking lot, headless of the puddles I splashed through.

I must have looked a fright at best or deranged at worst, sopping wet and running full-tilt for the door; the two deputies at the entrance made a grab for me, one touching a hand to his weapon.

"Officer Campbell," I pleaded, raising my hands up and slowing. "Please, I've got to speak with Officer Campbell."

The deputies shared a look. "Wait here," one said, disappearing into the doorway leaving his partner to watch the crazy lady standing in the rain.

"What do you want?" sour-faced as ever, Officer Campbell placed both hands on his hips and remained in the dry shelter of the building.

"Officer, that woman stole my phone." With one arm I pointed to Mamasan in the cruiser, never looking away.

"Miss Rivers, a charge of theft is not even a drop in the bucket amongst the crimes I plan to charge that woman with. Now, go wait in the car." He turned.

"Wait. I need it." I begged. "Please, did someone get it off of her? Do you have it? It's important."

"You young people and your blasted technology obsession." Officer Campbell stomped toward me. "I won't have my investigation interrupted for this nonsense."

"You don't understand. I have Regina's confession to the kidnapping recorded."

Chapter 29

"Thank God we're almost home!" Sam did a little happy dance in the passenger seat of my truck.

"I know. Who knew two days away could be so exhausting?"

"I still can't believe you forgot you had an app on your phone that records all of your calls. We could have handed that recording to the police right away and saved ourselves a lot of close calls."

Shrugging, ignoring the embarrassment tinging my cheeks, I played it off. "Then we would have missed all the action."

"Good. I'm done with action. Heck, I'm done with action movies, action figures, the word action, all of it!"

I grinned to see Sam struggling to hold a straight face. Her sunny disposition would be back in full force in no time.

"Do you want me to take you home or stop by the bakery?" I asked her.

I glanced over to find her giving me the one raised eyebrow look. I laughed.

"The bakery!" we said together.

We drove past the front of the shop, pleased to see a small crowd inside so close to closing, before parking in the back lot.

In the back, Flo hauled two small garbage bags to the dumpster. I waved as Sam called a hello. Flo nodded and smiled.

"It's still bothering me that her business is doing badly," I whispered to Sam. "We have to do something."

The back door swung open, taking us by surprise.

"You're back!" Victoria skipped over and wrapped us up in a hug. "I'm so glad you're back. Piper, you have to try this incredible cookie. Also, I had no idea how hard it is to bake all the time. My feet are killing me. Do your feet kill you, too? How was your trip? Did everyone like the desserts?"

"Whoa! Slow down, Victoria." Sam smiled and hugged the girl again. "Are you okay?"

"Who me? Sure, I'm fine. Quite fine. I was a little tired yesterday but then Millie made me some coffee and so that helped. I've had lots of coffee today. I accidentally spilled some coffee in the cookies actually, but then they were delicious so I ate those with my coffee drink, too. Come on, I want you to try them."

With her feet flying as fast as her words, Victoria pulled us into the kitchen and promptly deposited us on stools. I shook my head.

"Someone is way over-caffeinated," Sam whispered.

"Yep," I agreed watching Victoria dish cookies up onto plates which nearly went flying when she whirled around and speed-walked them to us.

The cookie presented prettily on the plate, a nice tan color with beautiful drizzles over the top. "What flavors are those?" I asked, pointing to the stripes zig-zagging across the cookies.

"Milk chocolate and caramel," Victoria answered.

"I can't wait to taste them!" Sam picked up a cookie and took a large bite. As she chewed, her eyes grew wider and wider.

Curious, I nibbled a tiny bite, barely more than a crumb, from my cookie. The caramel coated my tongue in a pleasant taste for a moment before an incredible jolt of coffee flavor took over. How it was physically possible to fit that much coffee into a mere morsel, I had no idea. No wonder Sam's face registered such shock – she had nearly half a cookie in that one bite.

"Wow," I kept my tone casual as I looked up at Victoria. She bounced on her toes, hands clasped in front of her, looking as eager as a puppy for praise. "Tell me how you made these."

"Sure. I had a plain ol' shortbread cookie dough all mixed up this afternoon and stopped to drink some more coffee. I sat drinking my coffee and staring at the dough trying to decide if I should jazz it up any, when Millie started talking right beside me. I didn't even know she had come in the kitchen so I jumped about a mile high. That's how I made the cookies."

I cocked my head sideways, as if maybe hearing the words a different direction would make sense of them.

Sam must have been puzzled as well; after swallowing several gulps of water, she asked, "Victoria? How did shortbread cookies become coffee cookies? What did you add?"

"My whole double espresso," she answered as if it were the most obvious thing in the world. "I spilt it all in the batter when Millie scared me. I thought about throwing it out, but decided to stir it in and see what happened after I baked it." She smiled. "Now, tell me – what do you think?"

"Lots of coffee flavor," Sam said.

"Very strong." I nodded as I tried to hide the rest of my cookie under a napkin. "Good idea to add the milk chocolate and caramel stripes."

"Thanks!" the girl jumped up and down.

"Have you been drinking double espressos like that all day?"

Victoria shook her head up and down at me. "Yes. Delicious. Didn't get sleepy once." She continued to talk at the speed of light and I felt bad for the poor girl. It would probably be days before she felt sleepy again.

Echoing my thoughts, Sam stood and looped arms with Victoria. "I think it is time for a cup of chamomile tea. Come on, I'll make you my favorite blend."

I left them to it and pushed through the swinging door into the café part of the bakery. "Hey Millie," I greeted the girl as she turned from wiping down the counter.

"Hi! I didn't know you guys were coming tonight. How did it go?"

"Fairly well," I hedged. "How did things go here?" I looked out past the counter to the cluster of people at tables and my jaw dropped.

No more white table tops met my eyes. Instead, an astounding array of colorful cookies and cupcakes showed on every surface. Speechless, I walked around the counter and touched the closest table, feeling of the paint, convinced that my eyes must have deceived me.

"Thanks so much for letting me use the bakery for my art project," Millie joined me and blushed. "I couldn't believe it when Gladys told me you said yes. What do you think?"

What I thought is that Gladys and I really have to have a talk about clear communication.

Millie didn't need to do her homework in the bakery as I believed; no, she transformed the bakery through her homework.

I said the only thing I could say. "It's...magnificent." And it was. Millie had talent and she had turned plain tables into true works of art. Cookies danced the conga, cupcakes sported frosting of every shade, and sprinkles spiraled around and throughout it all, a veritable dessert celebration. I wandered slowly around, taking them all in. Not a single table sported the same scene.

"I'm so glad you like it. I've been worried. If you want me to take it off or paint over them, please, just tell me."

"I love them! How in the world did you get all of these painted in a single weekend?" I asked her.

Millie only ducked her head and smiled. "I love to paint," she shrugged her shoulders.

Looking around, I noticed something missing. "Where is Gladys?"

"She left early for her cooking lesson."

"Cooking lesson? Why would she need a cooking lesson?"

"Who's having a cooking lesson?" Sam asked as she and Victoria joined us, large cups of steaming chamomile tea in their hands.

"Gladys. She's been going to lessons at the place that has classes for seniors."

Sam raised her eyebrow at me and I shook my head. For the life of me, I couldn't figure out why Gladys would be at a cooking lesson.

Chapter 30

"Haven't we done enough sneaking around this weekend?" Sam asked me half an hour later. The girls insisted they could handle cleanup and closing up shop which left the two of us free to go see about this cooking lesson of Gladys's.

"We are not sneaking around," I lowered my voice as we opened the doors to the Senior Citizen's Center. "We are simply checking out a new class in our community and letting our friend know we are home safe."

"Do you expect me to believe that?"

"Of course not, now come on." Turning down a hall to the right, we followed the sounds and smells of food, and of course the well-marked signs reading *Fab-ulous Foods* in large print, to the kitchen.

"Oh. My. Gosh." Sam whispered.

I could only nod. We had solved the mystery of the cooking class. Gladys, decked out in cocktail dress, zebra-print apron, and heels, stood next to none other than Chef Fabio as he extolled on about the fine art to a souffle in his magnificent French accent.

Backing slowly away from the door, Sam and I made an inconspicuous exit. "Should we tell her we know?" I asked as we re-entered the foyer.

Sam quirked her lips up to the side, thinking. "Hmm. Maybe not just yet."

"You know, this explains the fine French dining she created for dinner the other night."

"True. Since you still have to drive me home, why don't you just crash at my place tonight?"

"Deal." Exhausted, I didn't look forward to the drive out to Sam's much less turning around and driving back into town to my apartment. Stifling a yawn, I chuckled. "I sure hope some of that espresso wore off for Victoria by now."

"No kidding. When it does, she'll probably sleep a full eighteen hours. I think it is good we are giving them a few days off before asking if they want to be part-timers." Sam said. She and I had discussed the situation at length on the drive back to Seashell Bay today. The girls would be fun to have around for the rest of the summer if they said yes. I smiled, thinking of Millie's art project tables; there might be more decorating in the Ooey Gooey Bakery's future.

Silence encompassed us for most of the trip to Sam's condo. The garage on Griff's side was shut when we arrived and I wasn't about to go peeking in windows to see if he was home. Hauling Sam's bags up the stairs and into the living room, we dropped them in the middle of the floor and left them.

"Night," I called to Sam as I carried my toiletry bag into the guest bathroom. She waved and disappeared into her bedroom. After a quick shower, I snuggled under the cool sheets, eyelids drifting shut. Dancing cookies filled my dreams and sleep was sweet.

Chapter 31

The alarm went off an extra hour early the next morning. I rolled over and swiped the button to silence the cuckoo bird melody on my phone. Dressing in a flash, I tiptoed to the kitchen and made two cups of green tea. Moments later, Sam joined me.

"You've had enough jeans and tees, I see." I smirked at my friend. A bright smile greeted me in return as she strolled over to the counter and picked up her tea glass. Dressed in a fashionable white and black dress, she looked more suited to the dreaded dinner party next month than to a day at the bakery.

"Have to make a good impression on our customers; we've been gone a lot recently, after all."

"Right," heavy sarcasm made the word roll slowly from my mouth. "Whatever you say. I'm heading in to see if we have to make new dough or if Victoria left some ready to bake yesterday." Getting up, I strode to the couch and sat down to slide on my sneakers.

"I'm right behind you," Sam said.

Taking the stairs two at a time, I jogged to my truck and took off for work. Excitement bubbled inside of me and a goofy grin split my face, surprising me at how much I had missed the bakery in only two days.

I pulled up in the back lot to find Griff's truck parked next to the back door. He stepped away from the building where he leaned against the wall and waited for me. The goofy grin grew.

"Hey stranger," I smiled, unlocking the back door. Griff followed me inside. "If you make a habit of showing up this early, I'm going to assume you want a job," I joked.

"Maybe I'm just taking my responsibilities as official taste-tester more seriously."

"Then you will be disappointed to learn we hired a replacement for you just last week."

He arched an eyebrow at me. "Oh really?"

"Yep," I nodded as I slipped an apron over my head. "Gladys."

Griff laughed out loud. "I guess I'll have to apply for a new job then. The one I'm thinking of has everything to do with you and very little to do with this bakery though." He grew serious.

"And just what would this job involve?" I pursed my lips, tapping a finger on my chin, the perfect picture of contemplation.

"It's going to be a tough one, very demanding," he said with a mock frown.

"Is that so?" I narrowed my eyes at him.

He nodded. "Yep. I have to be funny enough to make you laugh," he ticked off on his fingers. "Kind enough to help you in everything you need."

I made a show of looking in the walk-in fridge, hoping to cool the heat rising to my cheeks.

"Persistent enough to gain your attention more than these cookies," he added pointedly. I turned and stuck my tongue out, but continued listening. "Sneaky enough to catch you by surprise. And honest enough to make you realize how amazing you are."

I swallowed. "You might be in luck," I told him. "I think there is a position open for that kind of job."

Griff scooped me up and spun me around. Laughing, I held on tightly.

As he sat me on my feet again, Griff led me to a stool and we sat down. "There's one more thing," he said.

My pulse picked up as I waited.

"I'm going out with Kendra tonight."

Like a giant bubble that floated into a tree limb, my excitement popped and died. I leaned back and shook my head, trying to clear it of what I just heard.

"You're agreement with Deidra?"

Griff squeezed my hand. "Yes. Mother insisted I agree to take Kendra to dinner and I did. She even gave me an entire checklist including buying flowers, ordering wine, and other nonsense. I wanted to come here and tell you that I plan to take her out tonight, fulfill my debt to Mother and be done with it."

It made sense in a painfully twisted way. "What about Kendra?" I asked. I supposed I should feel sorry for the woman. I probably shouldn't feel hurt and jealous; try telling either of those things to my heart though.

"I'll explain everything to Kendra at dinner. Don't worry, I will not let her get the wrong impression. Not when you are the one who is right for me."

"Okay." I took a deep breath. It would be fine. "Griff, thank you for telling me."

"I'm only sorry I have to go at all," he said.

I stood and got to work scooping cookie dough onto sheets before a realization dawned. I turned and grinned at Griff.

"What?" he smiled back, reclining one elbow on the work table and looking at me.

"Did we just have a completely uninterrupted conversation about something important?"

He laughed, making me laugh as well.

Griff grabbed my hand, leaning toward me. I moved a step closer, gazing up at him. My eyes fluttered closed.

The back door opened, startling us apart, as Sam strode in. "What did I miss?" she asked, swinging her head back and forth between the two of us, which only made us double over and laugh more. *So much for uninterrupted.*

"Okay then," Sam rolled her eyes. "I'll just start some new cookie dough and pretend I'm not sharing my workspace with a couple laughing hyenas."

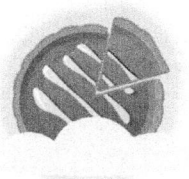

Chapter 32

"I guess I should go get Kendra's flowers." Griff wiped his chocolate-coated fingers on a napkin.

"Flowers for Kendra?" Sam asked sharply, frowning at her brother.

"You should take some cookies, too. Wait, I'll go with you to Flo's to pick some out." I tossed our trash into the can by the counter. "I just had a cool idea that I want to run by her to help her summer business pick up."

"Cookies? For Kendra?" Sam waved her arms at us. "What are you two talking about?"

I laughed. "It's a long story. Watch the counter while I'm gone?"

"Sure," she grumbled. "I want to hear this idea for Flo's business when you get back though. And then when my big brother here stops loafing in our bakery and goes to work, you and I are going to talk." She put her hands on her hips and tried for a stern expression.

"Yes ma'am." I saluted and she dissolved into smiles again. Walking to the door, I saw a now-familiar figure coming down the sidewalk. "I think this next customer is for you." I winked at Sam and headed next door with Griff. We smiled at Landon as he walked by, but continued forward on our mission.

Do you want to know more about Piper's plan to fortify Flo's flowers? Are you wondering how the date with Kendra goes? Curious about Gladys and the cooking classes? Ready to find out if Breaking Chains survives the colossal blow of corruption in their midst? Stay tuned for Ooey Gooey Bakery Mystery Book 3: Bake, Eat, & Be Buried.

Sign up for my newsletter to receive notifications of new releases by visiting: https://mailchi.mp/3ed2f71e303c/kbbnewsletterbookishinfo

Making a Difference, One Life at a Time

Human trafficking continues to take place all over the world, including in the U.S. where I live. In the creation of this book, I had the opportunity to speak with an individual who is one of many organizations working together to help release victims from the bonds of the trafficking industry, just like "Breaking Chains" in the book.

In our discussion, my friend Duncan told me about an organization in Houston, Texas called Elijah Rising with whom he and his church partner to pursue the goal of ending sex trafficking specifically.

Elijah Rising was founded in 2012 as a prayer gathering that grew into so much more. Now operating in three key areas, awareness, intervention, and restoration, Elijah Rising speaks up for those men, women, and children being forced or manipulated into the sex industry. Volunteers are part of interventions monthly, visiting the brothels, sex businesses, and streets or locations notorious for prostitution. Always honest, the volunteers introduce themselves and offer to pray over the individuals or their families. Often small gifts of soap, lipstick, flowers, or oranges (a symbol of good luck in Asian cultures) are given out with no strings attached. Free gifts, a rare commodity indeed, open the hearts of many of the recipients to ask why. Volunteers are able to make individuals feel valued as a person rather than an item. Cards, or even the gifts themselves, will have hotline numbers for the people to call and receive help to get out of the life.

Amazing, yes?

It doesn't stop there.

Restoration is the third part of Elijah Rising's heart. A residential program welcomes victims into housing, provides trauma-informed counseling, and caring, compassionate members of a community to help with the healing and support of survivors of sex trafficking.

For more information about Elijah Rising, to become a partner, or to donate visit https://www.elijahrising.org/about/.

Note from the Author

Thank you so much for taking the time to read Pastries, Pies, & Poison! I hope that you enjoyed more time getting to know Piper and Sam. If you are new to the series, check out Book 1 in the Ooey Gooey Bakery Mystery Series, Rest, Relax, Run for Your Life.

About the Author

Katherine Brown is a lover of books and weaver of words. Her first official publication was of two children's books in 2017, which has now grown into five books of the School is Scary series, soon to be finished with book six in 2019; however, she likes to think her career as a writer started when she sold her parents newsletters of articles about school and poetry for fifty cents per copy as a pre-teen.

Married to a wonderful husband and the mom of a smart, spunky stepdaughter, Katherine enjoys spending time with family and reading as many new books as she can get her hands on. Her YA series, the Ooey Gooey Bakery Mystery series, is ramping up in 2019 with book 1 Rest, Relax, Run for Your Life and book 2 Pastries, Pies, & Poison bot out during the first half of the year and book 3 well on the way.

Katherine also enjoys the challenge of telling an excellent story with few words. To check out some of her flash fiction and short story pieces, published online and free to read, follow the links below.

I'm the Last – Flash Fiction – Mercurial Stories
https://mercurialstories.wordpress.com/2018/09/08/week-24-the-last-stories/

But a Simple Breakfast – Flash Fiction – Mercurial Stories

https://mercurialstories.wordpress.com/2018/09/22/week-26-stories-breakfast/

Cloaked – Short Story – Enchanted Conversation Magazine (P.S. this is one of Katherine's favorites, another fairy tale remix)

http://www.fairytalemagazine.com/2018/12/cloaked-by-katherine-brown.html

Why I Write; How Can I Not? – Fiction Southeast Online

https://fictionsoutheast.com/why-i-write-how-can-i-not/

You can visit Katherine on:

Facebook

Amazon

Instagram

BookBub

www.katherinebrownbooks.com

Made in the USA
Monee, IL
01 July 2020